BROTHER

TO

BROTHER

BROTHER TO BROTHER

A MORMON LEADER AND A CATHOLIC BISHOP JOIN FORCES TO FIGHT FOR THE TRUTH

BY CHARLES MANLEY BROWN

BONNEVILLE BOOKS™

Springville, Utah

ISBN: 1-55517-750-6
e.1

Published by Bonneville Books
Imprint of Cedar Fort Inc.
www.cedarfort.com

Distributed by:

Cover design by Nicole Cunningham
Cover design © 2003 by Lyle Mortimer

1129 "Tell all the truth, but tell it slant" Reprinted by permission of the publishers and the Trustees of Amherst College from THE POEMS OF EMILY DICKINSON, Thomas H. Johnson, ed., Cambridge, Mass.: The Belknap Press of Harvard Univeristy Press, Copyright © 1951, 1955, 1979 by the President and Fellows of Harvard College.

Excerpt from IN THE BEGINNING by Chaim Potok, copyright © 1975 by Chaim Potok & Adena Potok, Trustees. Used by permission of Alfred A. Knopf, a division of Random House, Inc.

Printed in the United States of America
10 9 8 7 6 5 4 3 2 1
Printed on acid-free paper

Dedication

To: Grace Bowns Brown

In Memory Of

Charles Manley Brown, Jr.
1945-1991

William James Brown
1949-2001

Zina Lucile Brown King
1963-1988

Acknowledgments

Individuals who have been generous with their time and insights regarding the Mass include: Bernice Maher Mooney, archivist, Catholic Diocese of Salt Lake City; Members of the St. George Catholic Parish: the late Father Paul Kuzy, C.P.P.S., former Pastor; Sister Yvonne Hatt, CSC; Sister Ellen Mary Taylor, CSC; Timothy and Penelope Eicher.

Additional acknowledgments: The research librarians of the Dixie State College Library and the Washington County Library, St. George, Utah, were very helpful. In addition several individuals have made significant contributions to the completion of this novel through reading, editing, and reacting to the manuscript. They include my wife, Grace B. Brown, Douglas and Elaine Alder, Lavina Fielding Anderson, Pat Baum, Gerald Bowns, Hugh and Marilyn Brown, Dean and Marsha Burdick, Jack Callister, Carol Frost, JoAnn Hancey, Carolyn McDonald, David Nuffer, Gary Poll, Howard D. Swainston, Linda Taylor, Gary and Carole Terry, Lorraine O. Thomas, and Ralph and Mary B. Woodward. Their generous and thoughtful reactions have helped beyond measure.

To the Reader

This novel is set late in the first quarter of the twenty-first century for one reason only: to sidestep the reader's inevitable tendency to see current General Authorities in the personae created here. All characters are my own creation.

Although the question of forging religious documents may seem borrowed from the 1980s, tensions over interpretation of Mormon history could come from any period. Because of its setting in the future, some readers might place this book in the genre of science fiction, but I give events only a gentle nudge in that direction.

CHAPTER ONE

IN THE BEGINNING

Friday, 24 July 2020

Al Trask wasn't there yet, but then Sherman Drake and Mitchell Potter were a little early. They parked in front of the office/laboratory of Bernard Horne, Ph.D. Next door in the strip mall was a shoe repair shop. On the other side was the Yogurteria. Horne's sign read: "Forensic Analyst: Document Verification."

Drake wiped his palms on his pants. It had been two months since they'd handed over the document. He was sure Horne would confirm its authenticity. And then? He, Sherman Drake, would be on every telecast around the world explaining how he had yanked out the keystone of the Mormon Church. Or was it the cornerstone? He could never remember what Joseph Smith had called it. Whichever, nobody would ever again call the Book of Mormon the most correct book Joseph had claimed it to be. At least, not with a straight face.

He glanced at his chronometer. Five to ten, 24 July 2020, the anniversary of the day Brigham Young and his Mormon pioneers entered the Salt Lake Valley. He grinned at Potter. "Prepare to see your sacred ancestors spinning in their graves, Mitch," Drake smirked.

"Maybe. At any rate in a few minutes either we'll be dead in the water or the Mormon Church'll be dead in its tracks."

"Good mixed metaphor, Mitch. Should we wait any longer for Al Trask?"

"Let's give him five more minutes. It's too hot out here."

Monday, 11 May 2020

Sherman Drake's wrist alarm beep-beeped him awake at 6:30 a.m. He was quiet in the bathroom so as not to awaken Mitch. As he shaved, he looked carefully for any signs of graying. None. No sagging gut on his six-foot-two, 200-pound frame. Not bad for a thirty-two-year-old.

Okay, so he was a little over-anxious. Two hours before AmeriDelt flight 232 was called, he was sitting in O'Hare, trying to concentrate on the Chicago Tribune's crossword puzzle. Seven down, secret plan: *plot?* No, too short. *Scheme?* Yes. Unscheduled disaster: *catastrophe.* He checked the securely locked briefcase wedged between his left foot and the wall, the overnighter between his feet. Unexpected bonus: serendipity? Harriet, hot-lipped, hungry-handed Harriet, fit that one. Although he didn't like her whining, she had compensatory attributes.

In Salt Lake City, simultaneous with Drake's wrist alarm, Anthony J. Ririe—first counselor in the presidency of the Church of Jesus Christ of Latter-day Saints—heard the phone ring and woke with dread. Nobody called his private number with good news at 5:30 a.m. And this was the worst kind of bad news. The mission president reported that two of his sister missionaries, one from Edmonton, Alberta, one from Samoa, had been raped and beaten in Houston. One was dead. The other was in a coma with a skull fracture.

"Stay in the hospital with the survivor, President. I'll be in my office in a very few minutes. Keep this phone link open and download the parents' contact information to Brother Garrick. You still on the line, Garth?" he asked.

"Yes, sir," Garrick, head of Church Security, answered crisply. "I'll have the translators and both Area Presidents standing by when you get here." Garrick knew that while some previous presidents delegated all such notifications to the Area Presidencies, Ririe preferred to do it himself when he could.

"Shall I send a car around for you, President Ririe?" Garrick asked.

"No," Ririe growled firmly, pulling on his socks.

Marybeth was holding his jacket for him. He shrugged into it as he gave her the essential details. She looked stricken. "But you still have to eat, or you'll be exhausted by ten," she ordered. "Drink this, swallow this, and chew this on the way." She kissed his cheek as she opened the door for him.

He didn't argue. He washed the pill down with the orange juice and handed her back the glass. He took the scrambled egg sandwich, wrapped so he could hold it in one hand and steer with the other. He had a bite as he settled himself behind the wheel.

These things were never easy, especially if he found himself talking to a widow or to a nonmember parent. He took another bite at the stoplight. Bless Marybeth's heart. But it wasn't much easier with faithful, intact couples who responded with, "If this is God's will, we accept it." He never knew what to say. How would it help them if he told them what he always thought: "Why would the Lord *will* that a young woman trying to serve Him should be killed?" And no one, not even God, had ever answered his silent question.

He hadn't asked, but Garrick would have the bishops standing by, too. And it would have done him no good to tell Garrick not to call his secretary, Beverly Moore. Garrick had done this before—too many times.

Marybeth watched at the window as Tony drove away. She wished he would accept a security chauffeur. That way he could eat with both hands. Did he think it would be an admission that he was getting old? He was seventy, after all. Or scared? Or maybe it was just his way of resisting the smothering bureau-cracy, even though he made it work for him most of the time. As James D. Wood, the ninety-one-year-old president of The Church of Jesus Christ of Latter-day Saints, slipped toward death, Tony was adamant about not assuming presidential prerogatives, such as having his own driver.

At the gateway to the parking garage, the security scanner found no anomalies in his face or his car. His car slid onto the parking track, which whisked him to the underground entrance to the Church Administration Building. There it paused while he climbed out, then disappeared to be stacked in its slot. How else could a thousand vehicles fit into a space designed for 350?

As Ririe stepped off the elevator, Harry Thompson from the Missionary Department and Garth Garrick looked up quickly.

"Here's the background on the two Sisters," Thompson said as he handed over the file. "The bishops are standing by, and the translator is patched through. Both sets of parents are active members."

"Thanks, Harry," Ririe responded.

"Beverly's on her way in," added Garrick. "And here's the medical update."

Thank heaven for sat-phones, Ririe thought. *No matter where the parents are, they can hear the bad news together.* Nothing could be more agonizing than saying, "We have some bad news, but we need you to call your husband to come home first. Then call this number."

President Ririe's calls to the parents went better than he could have hoped. Breaking the news to the Samoan parents of the dead sister was the most difficult part of that conversation. Yes, a General Authority will be able to attend the funeral. No, he didn't know how long it would take to send her body to Samoa, but everything possible will be done to expedite things. Yes, a counselor in the Area Presidency would accompany the body. Yes, it is a comfort to know of God's eternal plan of salvation and to have the assurance of an eventual reunion on high. By all means, notify the extended family of this tragedy before they learn of it through the media.

The call to the parents in Canada in some ways was more difficult. But he got through it, thanks to the firm testimonies of the parents who were certain their daughter would recover. He then left it to the Area Presidencies in Houston and Edmonton, who were patched in to the call, to work out the details of flying the parents to their daughter's bedside.

CHAPTER TWO

PREP MEETING

President Ririe then went to his first meeting of the day—the First Presidency's daily preparation meeting. For the past three months, those in attendance had been the two counselors and the ever-present Secretary to the First Presidency.

They went through their agenda, fast and focused. Henry J. Cannon, the second counselor, five inches shorter than Ririe and a former corporate attorney, was a distinguished man, handsome and youthful at age fifty. He was a strong voice of logic and reason in these meetings. Deviation from the agenda and delay in resolving issues were never problems when Tony Ririe conducted in President Wood's absence. Wood had been given to reminiscing about how things were when he was first called as an apostle. This trait invariably lengthened the meeting and sometimes derailed progress. The agenda this day consisted primarily of financial issues—a prep meeting for the Church Expenditures Committee that afternoon.

By ten, President Ririe was back in his office, making and taking calls around the world: one to a Korean stake president, asking him to accept a five-year call as one of the temporary General Authorities; another to an area leader in Australia to express the condolences of the First Presidency over the death of his wife; and yet another to a mission president in Russia who had been misquoted by CNN as making some unfortunate comments about Russian history. Could he address a conference in Atlanta on medical ethics? No, but Mason du Gluck, an M.D. and Seventy would. The U. S. Senator from Massachusetts was going to have an operation for a cloned liver transplant. Would President Ririe give him a blessing? Yes. The Days of '47 Parade wanted him to ride in a hot air balloon towed forty feet off the ground and scatter salt-water taffy along the parade route. The governor of Utah had refused—too undignified. President Ririe's lips twitched. "Marybeth and I would love to," he announced firmly. He told Beverly to put it on his calendar and added, "Tell Brother Garrick that I absolutely will not discuss security risks."

At noon, he took the elevator down to the General Authorities' dining room, tastefully decorated in cream and blue with fresh flowers at every table. The food was excellent, served in modest portions. Not many of his compatriots took time for the vigorous exercise needed to keep their weight down, but he did. He appreciated the fact that the menu balanced low-fat and low-cal selections with fresh tastes and prime ingredients. Unfortunately the menu did not stop the steady invasion of gray from the beachhead of his temples upward. Fortunately, gray hair had not been a leadership disadvantage in the Mormon Church for more than a century.

He liked to drift up to any table with a vacant chair and ask to join the occupants. He kept a mental note of those with whom he had eaten most recently and those who might feel neglected. With informal questions and easy banter, he could take the pulse of his brethren in ways not possible in their business-focused meetings or in their monthly temple meetings.

After lunch he went over the recommendations of the Missionary Committee on additional men to be called as mission presidents. Most of these assignments had been made in the previous three months, but some vacancies needed to be filled immediately. He sighed. The Church was so large that most of the names were unfamiliar to him—even though he had been a Church leader for many years. Now and again he would recognize the name of someone whose stake he had visited or whose reputation in the world of business or academia made him seem familiar. He checked them all off, hoping to heaven the screening had been thorough—nobody under indictment for securities fraud, nobody running guns on the side. Their names would be on the agenda of the next Missionary Committee meeting.

At 2:30, after a link call, he drove to the home of Joseph R. Lund, president of the Quorum of the Twelve, who, at age ninety, was one heartbeat away from becoming the next President of the Church if the voice of tradition decided as it always had.

Tony Ririe genuinely loved President Lund. He'd seen him handle many difficult situations with grace and dignity. He'd seen him exercise his ecclesiastical authority firmly but with the true spirit of Christ—a spirit of forgiveness, a spirit of understanding, a spirit of reaching out to the individual. Ririe also was painfully aware of the health problems Joseph Lund was facing. Although he could no longer stand alone, he could walk a few feet with the aid of a walker. He still lived in the home he had occupied for forty years, thanks to the selfless service of his widowed daughter, Margaret Lund Perry, who had moved into that home following the death of her mother six years earlier.

Ririe was grateful that Joseph Lund's mind was as keen as ever. President James D. Wood, in contrast, was sometimes confused and unresponsive, as a result of age plus his most recent stroke. His islands of lucidity were unpredictable. Ririe knew he must keep Joseph Lund in the information loop. Who knew when he'd become the Church's chief decision maker?

After discussing many confidential matters, Lund asked, "And President Wood?" It was the ritual question. Ririe answered, "No marked change really. No worse, no better."

Lund nodded thoughtfully. Ririe began shuffling his papers together.

"Tony," Lund mused, "I'm not sure the Lord wants me to be President Wood's successor."

Ririe was startled. "That's a very surprising statement, Joseph."

"I've been giving a lot of thought to what I should do, if I outlive President Wood," continued Lund.

"I've always felt we should leave that up to the Lord, Joseph."

"So have I until quite recently, but I'll continue to make it a matter of prayer. The Lord doesn't answer questions we don't ask. I'm asking." Lund looked at Ririe gravely, then smiled. "Thanks for coming, Tony. You do more for me than any of my doctors."

CHAPTER THREE

SHADOW OF DOUBT

Monday, 11 May 2020

Passengers aboard the Boeing 797 heard the captain announce, "Those of you on the right can see Evanston, Wyoming, as we continue our descent toward the Salt Lake International Airport. The Great Salt Lake will be visible very shortly. We should be on the ground in less than fifteen minutes."

Sherman Drake, seated in 15J, was hoping to see downtown Salt Lake City on final approach. Luck was with him. They'd be landing south to north. After the jet had made two left turns, circling the southern tip of the Great Salt Lake, he could see the high-rise office and apartment buildings that dominated the central city skyline. Then he spotted the Mormon temple, visible for only a second or two, among its taller neighbors. He tried to track South Temple Street east, as far as the Cathedral of the Madeleine, his destination once on the ground.

As the giant airliner taxied to its gate, Drake switched off his TV monitor and clutched his briefcase even tighter. He remembered having seen an old movie in which a mad passenger clutched a similar case containing a bomb. *Well*, he thought, *I have a bomb, too! I wonder when it will go off?* With his overnight bag in one hand and the briefcase in the other, he went directly to the monorail terminal. It whisked him at 100 MPH to the only stop between the airport and downtown Salt Lake City. There he walked 100 yards to the Budget Car Rental office to pick up his reserved American-made

Toyota-Electric. While waiting for his "instant" paperwork to be processed, he purchased a copy of the local newspaper, the *Deseret Tribune*. Below the masthead was the date: 11 May 2020.

His overnight bag went in the trunk, but Sherman Drake put his briefcase in the passenger seat and threaded the seat belt through its handle. He drove two blocks south and turned east onto South Temple Street.

May was a good month in Salt Lake City. Trees were in full leaf but still bright with newness. Lilac bushes nodded purple and white. Guests in the ring of high-rise hotels could look down on Temple Square with its temple and tabernacle, set off by vivid beds of pansies and tulips.

Nearly 175 years before, on a hot July day, Brigham Young had led his little band of Mormon pioneers into what was to become the Salt Lake Valley—the center of a vast religious and corporate empire.

Sherman Drake looked to his left as he drove east past the temple. The still controversial Main Street plaza was bright with umbrella tables. He glanced at 47 East South Temple, the Church Administration Building. The Church of Jesus Christ of Latter-day Saints headquarters was barely big enough for the First Presidency and the Twelve, which made it a virtual shrine for the faithful. More than a century old, it looked like a cross between a Roman monument and a center for Supreme Court justices. Built in 1914, its interior had been renovated three times, but the exterior with its twenty-four partial columns looked just the same. Behind it stood the twenty-six-story office building that housed a fraction of the ever-expanding bureaucracy of the Mormon Church.

If you only knew what I know! He caressed his briefcase. Three blocks east he swung into the parking lot of the Cathedral of the Madeleine.

Sherman Drake had planned his meeting with Patrick J. Donavan, the Bishop of the Catholic Diocese of Salt Lake City, with great care. His choice of shirt, tie, and jacket leaned toward shades of brown and tan. He had telephoned Donavan two days earlier and had cryptically told him, "You don't know me, sir. My name is Sherman Drake. I live in the Chicago area. I have a fully documented manuscript in my possession that will blow the lid off the Mormon Church, and I want to make a gift of it to the Catholic Church. Please be available at the Cathedral in the late afternoon the day after tomorrow. I will tell you more at that time." Drake had hung up before Donavan could respond. He was sure Donavan was waiting for him on tenterhooks.

Drake asked a passing priest for directions and was surprised to learn that the bishop's office was in the Pastoral Center, across the courtyard from the cathedral. The receptionist sitting just outside the bishop's office referred him to the office of the bishop's secretary. *Did he have an appointment?* The middle-aged but still pert secretary wanted to know.

Sherman had been practicing his approach—mysterious but macho. "Please tell him Sherman Drake, the man with the manuscript, is here. I just flew in from Chicago. He's expecting me."

The secretary rose, went to Donavan's office, and gave him Drake's message. Donavan, who was running a CD simulating earthquake damage to the state's parochial schools, grunted in exasperation. "Show him in, and call me in three minutes to remind me that I must leave for an important appointment."

He switched to a screen-saver of a Tahitian beach as Drake entered, and gestured him to a seat.

"Your Excellency, it's a pleasure and an honor to meet you, sir." Drake was deferential as he perched himself on the very edge of the chair. His persona was now that of the humble disciple.

Donavan nodded. "And your manuscript?"

"Sir, it will disprove Joseph Smith's account of how the Book of Mormon came to be published," Drake responded eagerly.

Donavan nodded again, face expressionless. "And how will it do that?"

Drake pulled a large manila envelope from his briefcase. "I have here," he breathed, his tone reverent and sly simultaneously, "a fully authenticated manuscript dating to before Joseph Smith's birth. It corresponds to the Book of Mormon to a most remarkable degree. I want to see the Mormon Church exposed for the fraud it is. It seems to me to be a project in which you may appropriately interest yourself, Your Excellency."

Donavan swung his chair around abruptly, leaving Drake staring at the back of his head. *Aha*, he thought. *He's really interested!* Drake glanced around the office. One of the photographs showed the bishop in tennis whites, a considerably younger man, his arm draped around the shoulder of his partner. Both were grinning triumphantly. He's someone who understands competition, thought Drake. The partner reminded him of someone—but Donavan had swung back to face him.

"And just what is your plan?"

Drake spoke eagerly. "I want you to present this document to your most learned scholars in Rome or wherever. I want them to authenticate it for themselves. Then His Holiness could make the facts known to the world and issue a stinging denunciation of this religious hoax."

"How did you get this manuscript?"

"That's an involved story, Your Excellency. But I assure you that it's authentic."

Donavan's buzzer sounded. He lifted the receiver.

"Your three minutes are up, sir," his secretary told him.

"Yes," responded Donavan. He kept the phone to his ear for about fifteen seconds, and then repeated, "Yes."

Donavan stood. "You must excuse me, Mr. Drake. I have received an emergency summons."

Drake was standing too, waving the envelope and trying to speak, but the bishop kept talking as he moved around the desk, took Drake by the elbow, and ushered him firmly to the door.

"Yes, please leave your document with me. Give your telephone number to my secretary. Ask her to arrange a time when we can meet again in a few days. Thank you for coming by. Good day, sir."

The bishop plucked the envelope from Drake's hand, closed the door behind him, and quickly called his secretary on the phone, not the intercom, instructing her to make the appointment no sooner than four days hence. When he was certain Drake had left the building, Bishop Donavan placed a call to his old friend, Tony Ririe, at Mormon Church headquarters. While waiting for the call to go through, Bishop Donavan reflected. Drake was certainly smarmy and unpleasant, but could this document be what he claimed it to be? *Time will tell*, he thought.

Inside the neo-classical building that Drake had passed earlier, Tony Ririe was about to begin what he thought would be his next-to-last meeting of the day. He walked briskly from another meeting toward his office in the southeast corner of the first floor.

Rosalie Torres, managing director of the Public Relations Department, and two sober-suited staffers were waiting. It was a large room, heavily decorated with tastefully framed family photos, mementos from world travels, paintings, certificates of appreciation from various dignitaries, and a magnificent globe of the world. Ririe shook hands with all of them and briskly asked Rosalie Torres to offer an invocation.

Immediately after the "Amen," Ririe announced, "Although we have about thirty days to decide, we should make contingent arrangements now, subject to future events." He sounded pompous, even to himself. He hastily added, "I'm going in the balloon, no matter what, so it's really a question of deciding how many we want to put in the open limo."

Rosalie Torres grinned. "Well, you certainly made Jingo Woodruff's day. He was so excited when he told me you agreed that he sounded forty feet above the parade route himself." She sobered, "But why do we need to decide now? What difference will it make if we postpone the matter for a few weeks? Surely, if President Lund is well enough at the time, which doesn't seem likely, he'll ride in the limo. If not—and if Brother Garrick can't talk you out of that balloon—then President Cannon will."

"It's important to decide now, Sister Torres, because of the implications of appearing indecisive both now and later," Anthony Ririe declared in his characteristically forceful manner. "Every car, float, band, and horse group—about 140 in all—will have been given a place in the parade no later than June 15. Such advance planning is absolutely essential for an undertaking as huge and involved as this one."

"But surely the presidential car can be given a place without specifying its occupants," Rosalie countered. "It's certainly spacious enough to seat President Lund and whoever."

Tony Ririe's eyes fell on the flashing light on his telephone. Another emergency. He usually never interrupted meetings for phone calls. He lifted a finger with an apologetic glance at Rosalie.

"Yes, Beverly?"

"It's Bishop Patrick Donavan," Beverly's voice was urgent,

low. "He says it's very important."

"Just a minute," he told her. He looked at Rosalie. "Is there any reason not to treat this as a simple matter of protocol?"

She shook her head, her black curls bouncing. "I'll put together two scenarios: Lund with Cannon, and Cannon without Lund. We can add and subtract relatives as needed to fill the limousine."

He nodded, grateful for her initiative and speed. Her two staffers were already standing up as he apologized, "I need to take this call."

Rosalie closed the door softly behind her.

CHAPTER FOUR

BISHOP PATRICK DONAVAN

"All right," Ririe quietly told Beverly.

"Patrick, you old son of a gun. How are you?" he exclaimed jovially, grinning despite the urgency he felt. "And what's going on in the diocese today?" Ririe and Donavan had gone to high school and the University of Utah together and had developed a respect for each other and for the depth of their respective religious convictions. Now that one was a top Mormon leader and the other Bishop of the Catholic Diocese of Salt Lake City, their opportunities to meet informally and talk about neutral matters were rare indeed. Even more rare were their discussions of matters of faith.

"Tony, I must see you immediately—confidentially and very privately. I'm onto something potentially devastating. Something that could directly affect the future well-being of your church and perhaps my own, as well."

Ririe, reading the tone of Donavan's voice more than his words, responded decisively. "I'll be less conspicuous at your place than you in mine. You have a small room where we can meet privately?"

"Yes. Drive to the north parking lot. I'll meet you there. And bring your copy of the Book of Mormon."

With studied calm and the desk copy of his scriptures in hand, Ririe walked past Beverly's post and told her a minor emergency would keep him out of the office for the rest of the day. Since it was already five o'clock, his calendar was clear except for the meeting of the Expenditures Committee. "Please ask President Cannon to have me excused. See you tomorrow."

He realized Beverly would be puzzled, but there was nothing he could do about that at the moment.

As Tony Ririe drove out of the circular exit ramp, he did not notice the nondescript sedan following him at a discreet distance.

He thought back to when he had first met Pat Donavan. East High School, one of the oldest in the school district, served part of the affluent east side of the city where many of the prominent families clustered. Mayors, governors, and not a few of the elite in the medical and legal professions had prepared for university work there. Catholics attended the academically solid and well-respected Rowland Hall parochial school, but Pat had enrolled at East High and had been in Tony's tenth-grade homeroom class. Both had tried out for the school tennis team, and both had excelled. As a doubles team they had taken all-state honors their last two years at East High. Both had excelled academically as well and continued to be star tennis doubles at the U. In fact, Patrick Donavan was one of the reasons Tony Ririe had decided to attend the University of Utah rather than Brigham Young University in Provo.

Ririe had often visited the Newman Center at the U with Pat, just as Pat had frequently attended Institute of Religion lectures and activities with him. Both got along well with each other's friends and enjoyed the amicable and interminable wrangling over doctrinal differences. Tony had never given up a secret hope of getting Patrick to see the truth and was pretty sure that Patrick cherished the same secret hope where he was concerned.

He was right. As Bishop Donavan walked toward the exit of the Pastoral Center closest to the parking lot, carrying the large envelope casually under his arm, he thought fondly of Tony Ririe. *Why can't a man as intelligent as Tony Ririe see how preposterous his religious views are?*

Ririe pulled into the cathedral's north parking lot just as Bishop Donavan emerged from a side door. After a quick handshake, Donavan guided his friend to a small chapel where they could talk in complete privacy. As the two sat on the bench, Donavan plopped the envelope between them.

"I haven't opened this yet, but this is what my call was all about. One Sherman Drake, describing himself as from the Chicago area, gave it to me less than an hour ago. He claims that this document is more than 200 years old, that it has been fully documented, and that it will prove that Joseph Smith did not write the Book of Mormon."

Ririe eyed the envelope with distaste, "There's no way that document can be genuine."

"How do you know that without even looking at it?" queried Donavan.

"I just know," Ririe asserted. "But let's look."

Donavan and Ririe shifted a bit so as to be able to view the pages as they sat side by side. At a nod from Donavan, Ririe slid the manuscript out of the envelope and read aloud the first hand-written lines: "'I, Nephi, having been born of goodly parents, therefore I was taught somewhat in all the learning of my father.' " Ririe stopped. "Well, that part's right." He flipped open his triple combination and handed it to Donavan, pointing to the first verse.

Donavan put the triple on his knee and looked soberly at his old friend. "Logically, Tony, there are two possibilities. Either this is the source of Joseph Smith's translation, or these pages represent someone's attempt to create a manuscript designed to have the appearance of such a source."

"Pat, you know I can't accept your first possibility; that leaves us with the second." Tony flipped the manuscript to its last page and read aloud. "'And now, O man, remember and perish not.' Those words are found in Mosiah, about a third of the way into the Book of Mormon. That means, of course, we have less than half of the possible total. Where's the balance?"

"Good question, if there is a balance," Donavan replied.

"Pat, can you let me take this to my people for an examination?"

"I was just thinking the same about my people. Could we divide these pages into equal piles, one for each of us? By the way, time is an important factor—I agreed to meet this Drake in four days. Can you do what you need to do by then?"

"I could get a good start through some of our BYU people. Can you?"

Donavan nodded: "A priest on my staff did his dissertation on the Book of Mormon at Notre Dame. He probably knows more about the Book of Mormon and its history than any non-Mormon in the country—possibly more than many Mormons." Tony noticed Pat's grin.

Pat took the first half and returned the second half to the envelope. Tony suggested, "Since time is an issue, how about having our respective experts approach their tasks from different angles—internal evidence on the one hand and the paper and ink tests on the other?"

"Good idea," Donavan replied. "But I don't have any forensic experts on my staff."

"I'll tackle that part then," Ririe decided

Patrick looked earnestly at his friend. "You may be right when you say this thing's a fake, Tony. But what'll happen if our experts authenticate it?"

"They won't, Pat. I know that in my heart of hearts. But that doesn't mean we'll do anything less than the most rigorous and objective examination possible."

"We have four days, Tony," Donavan declared. " I believe the ball's in your court—you have the most to lose. You and your people will want to consider your possible options most carefully, but I don't need to tell you that. I feel that my options currently are limited to examining the content of what we have. If I stall Drake too long, he may demand the return of his document and take it somewhere else. Anyway, I'm ready and anxious to help in any way you think I can."

"Pat, I can't tell you how much I appreciate what you're doing," Ririe nodded warmly. "I'll consult with some of my people while you do the same with yours, and get back to you in two days."

"Shall we meet here?" Pat asked.

"Yes, this is a good place. If some of my colleagues knew where we're meeting, they might argue that this is not neutral ground. But privacy is far more important than protocol right now. And, as I have told you many times, you're like a brother to me."

"I feel the same way about you, Tony. Nevertheless, for a long time I've wanted to ask you how you know yours is the one and only true church?"

This question seemed to come from left field, but Ririe answered quickly, "In a word, Pat, it's faith. May I ask you the same question?"

"My answer's the same as yours, Tony. But how can faith lead us in such opposite directions?"

"Probably because our starting points are so far apart. Even though Christ is the central figure in both cases, we see him in different ways. The two millennia of Catholic history have molded a belief structure that is impenetrably secure. The history of the LDS Church, on the other hand, while it subsumes some of your Catholic beliefs and history, is less than two centuries old."

"This probably isn't the time or place to continue our discussion," Bishop Donavan noted.

"I agree, but I hope we can dig more deeply soon."

"Let's do it, Pat—but after the matter of the mysterious document has been cleared up."

They discussed what the next steps should be and agreed to meet in two days for mutual progress reports. After a few more minutes of friendly reminiscence and bringing one another up to date on family and mutual friends, Bishop Donavan escorted President Ririe to the door. Tony Ririe drove directly to his home.

Bishop Donavan, carefully carrying his allotted pages, walked slowly back to his office, deep in thought. *If there's anything to this mysterious manuscript, what will become of my dear friend and brother?* He wondered further what more he might be able to do to help. He slept fitfully that night, but not before offering a special rosary for his dear Mormon friend, Anthony J. Ririe.

CHAPTER FIVE

MARYBETH

Marybeth Ririe, Tony's wife of forty-six years, had experienced a day easier than most, despite its depressing beginning thirteen hours earlier. There had been no meeting of the wives of the General Authorities, no requests for her to speak at a local Relief Society meeting, and only a few family e-mail messages to handle. She had time to wonder about her children and asked herself, *How do you help your son develop a better relationship with his wife without appearing to meddle?*

Then her thoughts turned to her husband. *How long can Tony handle the strain of running the Church without appearing to do so?* She knew President Wood wasn't the same dynamic leader he had been just a few months ago. She knew key decisions had to be made daily and that her husband had to make most of them. How she longed to get him away—to the family cabin on the Snake River in Idaho for two or three days fishing, away from the phone calls and the emergencies, large and small, that inevitably came to him in the operation of the Church worldwide. The two sister missionaries in Houston. An earthquake in Romania that had caused the collapse of a chapel full of worshippers. A bishop convicted by his DNA of child molestation. A stake president excommunicated following conviction on felony fraud charges. She was startled from these thoughts by the familiar sound of her husband's car pulling in to the garage.

"Tony, what brings you home this early?" Marybeth Ririe greeted him at the door. Her smile quickly faded. "Good heavens, you look like you've just seen a ghost!" She glanced at his loosened tie. Then she noticed the manila envelope under his arm. "Where's your briefcase?"

He smiled and kissed her cheek. "Briefcase? I must've left it at the office."

As they walked arm in arm into the house, Marybeth felt the first stirrings of real panic.

Marybeth Ririe wondered if she knew her husband as well as she should. Married well before the turn of the twenty-first century, they had worked together to finish their education, had five children, and supported each other in both tangible and intangible ways. Marybeth had assumed the traditional supportive role of full-time wife and mother while Tony, the more public half of their partnership, grew in his profession as an accountant and as he received additional callings in the Church, each more demanding than the last. Along the way, she'd learned when to probe and when to keep silent. Obviously, this situation called for the second skill.

Tony Ririe hung his jacket in the front hall closet, took off his tie, walked into the front den, and carefully placed the manila envelope on a table. Marybeth went to the kitchen and prepared two cups of hot Pero—still a favorite substitute for the otherwise ubiquitous coffee. As she placed his mug on the low table next to his recliner, she saw a look on his face she had never seen before. When she tried to describe that face to herself later she used the words *almost shaken, extremely agitated,* and *desperately frightened.*

"I've got a little more dinner prep to do in the kitchen, Tony." *A justified white lie,* she thought. Ririe nodded absently, but didn't reach for his cup. They'd shared their cups of Pero on many occasions, some trying, some routine, some very pleasant. That he didn't ask her to stay worried Marybeth almost as much as his expression. She carried her own mug back to the kitchen and tried to remember other very difficult moments.

She remembered the day she had read of the excommunication of a senior member of the Quorum of the Twelve—a group held collectively and individually in remarkably high esteem by the membership of the Church and only to a slightly lesser extent by the community at large. She recalled—and the recollection still brought a tremor of disbelief—the simple single sentence framed in black on the front page of the then *Deseret News*: "The First Presidency of the Church of Jesus Christ of Latter-day Saints announces the excommunication of Andrew M. Maddox for violating one of the Ten Commandments." Although Tony had been a member of the Quorum of the Twelve for just a few short months when this took place, he'd been an equal member of the disciplinary council that had pronounced the sentence on that venerated apostle. And she never learned from Tony any of the details of the offense, nor of the proceedings of the council—only that it had been a most difficult experience.

Is something similar now taking place? She recalled the nights, years before, when Tony had been a bishop of a large ward. He would come home and say, "We had a disciplinary council tonight. I hope we never need another." But there had been others, and Bishop Ririe had been drained each time. But he'd been tight-lipped. The few details Marybeth ever learned came through the ward grapevine.

She recalled later disciplinary councils when Tony had been a stake president. Then, too, Ririe had been circumspect in keeping all details of such proceedings to himself. But on none of those occasions had he ever looked as he did this night. She tried not to surmise what was troubling her noble husband, but she couldn't wrench her mind from the challenge. Another high-level excommunication? The appointment of a man totally unacceptable to Tony to a high position in the Church? The imminent death of the Prophet?

She remembered the night he'd come home to tell her of the death of a young missionary on the other side of the globe, of the telephone call to his parents—kind, faithful, loving souls who accepted "the will of the Lord" but whose lives would never be the same. She remembered happier moments, such as the day he'd told her about the decision to build even more temples throughout the world. And she recalled the many high council dinners she'd prepared when Tony had been a stake president—dinners at which she'd been complimented many times for her gracious hospitality. But what could be so distressing now? For a fleeting moment she even wondered, *Is my Tony himself in some sort of personal trouble?*

As she nursed her cup of Pero, her thoughts moved back. She thought of her faithful parents, mainly faithful brothers and sisters, her excellent education in the Salt Lake City public schools, and her days at the University of Utah from which she'd graduated summa cum laude.

She recalled the first time she'd seen Tony Ririe. He'd been playing tennis on an adjacent court and had flipped one of her tennis balls back when it landed near him. She'd responded with a semi-curtsy and a cheerful, "Thank you, kind sir."

She'd recognized him, of course—Tony Ririe, the tennis star. At twenty-four, this returned missionary who had served in Scotland was a senior and still single. When she mentioned his name to her parents, they told her she should try to arrange a mixed doubles match. She had. The tennis match turned into a perfect match. Although Tony had given up tennis years earlier, she could still hold her own on the court with any woman her age.

They'd been married in the Salt Lake Temple "for time and

all eternity." Her Uncle Fred had performed the ceremony. She and Tony had been dressed in white temple robes—robes not changed in style for 150 years.

She recalled some of the changes in the temple endowment ceremony she'd heard about. She'd been pleased at the most recent change that had brought out more of the direct teachings of the Savior. In her mind the changes emphasized the most important aspects of the gospel as taught by the Savior himself—the Sermon on the Mount and the two great commandments to love God and to love one's fellow beings. More importantly to her, the meaning of the atonement—that most important facet of the gospel—was made clearer.

Her thoughts then moved to their four-day honeymoon in Hawaii. More time for honeymooning hadn't been available because of their professional responsibilities—he as a new accountant, gathering experience to qualify as a CPA, and she with a valued teaching position. But, she reflected, their life together had been a continuous honeymoon. He'd always treated her with respect, trust, and care. Even though she'd never been his confidante about Church matters, he'd never communicated any sense of superiority. She knew of other women whose husbands dominated the marriage, belittled them, and always insisted that their needs take precedence. How fortunate she felt!

She reflected on teaching elementary school in Salt Lake City while Tony finished his MBA at the University of Utah. Later she'd supplemented the family income when necessary by doing substitute teaching. That necessity ended after a very few years as Tony worked his way up in the major accounting firm that hired him immediately upon his graduation. She recalled again her elation when he became one of the youngest full partners in the accounting firm; she also recalled her mixed emotions six months later when he was called to be a member of the Quorum of the Twelve Apostles, at age forty-three.

She thought of their five children—each one so different from the others.

She chuckled, recalling their eldest daughter's comment to Tony when she learned of his call as an apostle. "Now, Daddy," she'd warned, "you'll be adulated, praised, even fawned over, and told how great you are by friends and strangers alike. That won't hurt you one bit as long as you don't believe a word of it."

And now, she thought, as she washed her mug, *what could I possibly do to help my distraught husband? I can't pry or snoop or otherwise try to find out the source of his concern. But I can trust in him and in the Lord.* She bowed her head in silent prayer.

CHAPTER SIX

COULD THIS BE?

Ririe moved to a nearby table, leaving the Pero behind, and opened the envelope. He turned the pages slowly, recognizing the verses. He asked himself, *Could this be the source of Joseph Smith's Book of Mormon?* He almost shuddered at the thought. Although he was certain it was not, the thought nagged him.

I need two kinds of help right now—the Lord's and some expert's, Ririe decided. He knelt to invoke the help of the Lord. Then he considered where next to turn. This document, transmitted by his old friend, was so potentially devastating that Ririe momentarily lost his power to concentrate. It was as if he had suffered a physical shock. *But why am I thinking in those terms if I know the document is a hoax?* His mind was working again now. *But if it isn't a hoax its potential impact could be devastating not only to the Church, but possibly also to other churches as well, and perhaps to the future of Mormons in high-level positions in academia, government, and business. There I go again, vacillating.* He knew that the Church had withstood the Hofmann forgeries in 1986 and the Spaulding document of the nineteenth century. This new challenge would prove equally false. His faith simply permitted him no other answer. But he needed to marshal support.

First, with whom should he share this information? *President Wood? No, he was too far-gone mentally to be able to handle anything so strenuous. The other counselor, Henry Cannon? But Hank was on his way to Denver—first for a family vacation in the Rockies, then for an Area Conference the following weekend. Besides, Hank had a tendency to act before he'd thought things all the way through. Joseph Lund, the President of the Twelve? Possibly. Grant Belnap?* As the name came into his mind, his mental faculties sharpened and focused.

Grant Belnap, sixth in seniority in the Twelve, was steady, unflappable, dependable, and close-mouthed. He'd been educated at Harvard—undergraduate and then law school— and had made his mark in his profession. Furthermore, his testimony had weathered many severe storms, including the death of his wife in a tragic automobile accident two years earlier. "Grant Belnap is my man," Tony Ririe voiced aloud as he rose from his chair.

Marybeth opened the den door. "Did I hear you call, dear? Dinner is ready when you are."

"You eat, dear. My dinner can wait. I need to see Grant Belnap," he smiled strangely as he put on his tie, donned his jacket, picked up the envelope, and kissed Marybeth. "Don't wait up for me, but I know you'll leave something for me to eat later," he directed.

Marybeth Ririe had seen Tony wrestle with the devil before. She had complete faith in her husband and knew who'd be the victor. No, she wouldn't wait up for him, but she'd still be awake when he returned. Oh, how she yearned to hold him in her arms and to be held in his!

CHAPTER SEVEN

GRANT BELNAP

On his way to the Belnap home, Tony Ririe, engrossed in his swirling thoughts, again did not notice the nondescript sedan.

Grant's car was backing out of the driveway. Tony honked and waved, pulling to the curb. Fifty-nine-year-old Belnap turned off his engine and met Tony on the front steps.

"I was just going to see you, Tony," he declared without preliminaries. "We have a challenge—something I learned about just ten minutes ago. But you have something on your mind, too. Do you want to speak first?"

He unlocked the front door and ushered Ririe inside.

"Has your house been checked for bugs recently, Grant?" Ririe asked abruptly, as they headed for the den. The very idea of electronic eavesdropping was repulsive to Tony Ririe and his colleagues. But great power begets great animosity, and some with agendas of their own had tried to bug the phones and homes of certain church leaders. It was standard practice to de-bug the homes of the top fifteen or twenty Mormon leaders regularly. Devices were found rarely—but often enough to keep the practice going.

"Only last week, Tony."

"Good. Tell me what you meant when you said we have a challenge."

They settled into facing easy chairs. Grant didn't waste any time. "You'll recall my telling you about Harriet Hudson's persistent attempts to interest me in her romantically a few years back."

Tony Ririe did recall Harriet Hudson. She had been Belnap's secretary many years earlier when Grant Belnap had been senior partner in a prestigious local law firm and stake president in one of Salt Lake's wealthier suburbs. Because of her advances to him in the office, he gave her a choice of resigning or being fired. He had been kindly but absolutely unwavering as she denied, then cried, then exploded in anger, then begged for another chance. Finally she resigned. A few months later, she had confessed to her bishop, after he confronted her with information he had received to that effect, that she was indeed having an affair with a bishop's counselor in a nearby ward. The man's stake president excommunicated him, and Harriet's bishop excommunicated her. She had appealed that decision to Belnap, who was then her stake president. He had upheld the bishop's decision. She had moved from the state some months later and had not been seen in Salt Lake City for several years.

"She called me a few minutes ago. Says she can prove the Book of Mormon is false, that it's payback time, but that she could conceal that proof, if I'd make it worth her while. I told her I was just leaving for an appointment I couldn't defer and that I'd call her back. She's at a motel downtown. I was coming to see you when you arrived just now."

Tony Ririe felt as if he'd sustained another physical shock. Donavan wouldn't have mentioned the mysterious document to anyone. Donavan may have already enlisted the help of his priest but that couldn't be the source of the Hudson woman's information. Harriet Hudson must either know Sherman Drake or know whomever Drake had talked to.

"Grant, there's more to what you just told me than you know," Ririe observed heavily into the lengthening silence. "I came here to discuss this same challenge with you, not knowing, of course, that Harriet Hudson had called you. Pat

Donavan showed me the so-called proof only this afternoon, and I have half of it here in this envelope. A man named Sherman Drake from Chicago came to his office today claiming he had an authentic manuscript, dating back to before the birth of Joseph Smith, which is the basis of the Book of Mormon. He left that document with Pat who agreed to see him again in not more than four days. We looked at the document briefly and divided it between us. He'll have his people examine his part, and we must find the best person at BYU to do the same with mine."

Belnap was quick. "Then Harriet Hudson knows of this document. But how? Could she have some connection with Sherman Drake?"

"Do you know where Harriet Hudson moved after her excommunication?" Tony asked.

Belnap shook his head.

Ririe pulled himself together. "I need your advice, Grant. Do we inform Hank Cannon and the Twelve? Pat Donavan will want to know my suggestions for his next steps."

Grant glanced at the envelope. "Could I see the manuscript?"

Tony Ririe handed it over, and Belnap carefully turned the pages, pausing long enough to recognize a passage, then going on. Finally, he tapped the pages together and put them back in the envelope. He spoke decisively. "Tony, you should get our best person working on this—tonight, if possible. In my law practice, I always restricted any potentially damaging information to as few people as possible, but I recommend you bring in Hank Cannon. Counselors shouldn't have secrets from each other."

Ririe nodded. "That makes sense, Grant. Hank left this evening for Colorado and won't be back until Monday. I should be able to reach him through his secretary or through Church

Security. But who is the best qualified person to look at these pages?"

"I know just the man," Belnap said. "Robert McDonald works in the archivist's office in the Church Office Building. He's done forensic verification of many items submitted to the archives over the years. Good background with lots of contacts."

"See if you can reach him at home and ask him to come here."

Fortunately, McDonald lived in the downtown area and was at home. Within twenty minutes he was ringing Belnap's doorbell.

The two serious Church leaders swore him to secrecy, gave him the relevant background, and asked him to determine the authenticity of the ink and the age of the paper within forty-eight hours.

"Brethren, I appreciate your confidence in me. But I can't perform miracles," McDonald protested. "What you're asking usually takes weeks. Two days just isn't realistic."

Ririe responded, "I appreciate your candor and your expertise, Brother McDonald. But time constraints are very much part of the equation. Can you begin to get a hint as to the age of these sheets in that much time?"

"Yes, sir, a hint. But hints won't stand close scrutiny."

"We'll settle for a hint for now. Maybe we'll be able to give you more time later on. Take this manuscript, start where you think you'll be most likely to hit pay dirt, and get back to Elder Belnap privately here at his home. By the way, do you have what it'll take to do this job at your home? Good. We don't want any of your fellow-workers to know about this—that includes your former colleagues at the Y."

"Yes, sir. I'll do what I can, given the time constraints. What you've told me has really shaken me, but I propose to do my job with complete objectivity, irrespective of the outcome."

Ririe and Belnap nodded their agreement. As Robert McDonald carried the fateful envelope to his car, the two leaders sat looking at each other.

"Tony, perhaps we need to find out more about this Sherman Drake," suggested Belnap. "If he proves to be an authentic document dealer with a clean reputation, that's one thing. If he proves to be anything less, our job should be easier. Nevertheless, we mustn't be guilty of the fallacy of origin. However, all we have to go on is a name. In my law practice, we sometimes located people through their automobile license plates. Did you say that Drake just flew in from Chicago? Then he most likely has a rental car." Grant Belnap rubbed his forehead and temples with his fingers and thumbs as he thought out loud.

"Aha!" Tony exclaimed. "I wonder if he's ever been a member of the Church? If so, we should have some sort of record on him. I'll have that checked out first thing in the morning. Then we may have something solid to work on. Let's meet in my office tomorrow morning about seven, okay?"

"Sounds right to me, Tony. Now, why don't we try to get some rest? Tomorrow might just possibly be a bigger day than usual."

"You're the master of the understatement, Grant."

In the early hours of the next morning, Marybeth was awakened by her husband's voice saying, "Could this be the source of Joseph Smith's Book of Mormon?" She quickly realized that Tony was talking in his sleep. *Should I wake him up?* She decided to wait and then heard him ask himself, "Where did this document come from and where has it been all these years?"

CHAPTER EIGHT

HARRIET HUDSON

Monday, 11 May 2020

Harriet Hudson, drawing on her fourth cigarette, shifted her weight on the hard motel chair, fuming because she still had not received the call from Grant Belnap she had been expecting for nearly two hours. *Had it been a mistake to come back to Salt Lake City after all these years? And a mistake to think I could snare Grant Belnap? Maybe*, she thought, *revenge is enough—revenge on him for the death of my mother and on the Church for my excommunication. Oh well, Chicago has been good for me. Especially Sherman Drake.* As she crushed the stub, she coughed. She didn't wonder about the truth of the Word of Wisdom—science had long since demonstrated that. *So why do I smoke? Rebellion, conformity, stupidity, addiction!*

The ease with which she'd adapted to her Chicago environment and to the ways of the big city had surprised her. *Yes, Salt Lake is a big city, but I was essentially a small town girl. Still, it didn't take me long to move to shorter skirts and lower necklines.* She chuckled, recalling the clerk's comment as she preened in front of the mirror. "That's a biblical neckline: 'lo and behold.'" She then and there took as her motto the old saw: "If you've got it, flaunt it!"

Yes, that dress was indeed a departure from her previous wardrobe, mainly business suits. And her life, until she'd been forced to resign from Grant Belnap's employ, had been plain for the most part. Her legal secretary routine had also been plain, if not drab. Computer processing legal papers week after week became boring. Then she'd gone home each day to her mother, whom she loved, and her father, whom she hated.

Is that why I tried to seduce my married boss? Stupid, knowing he was a happily married man. I should've known he wouldn't jeopardize his marriage, his career, or his membership in the Church he so obviously loved.

No longer a member of the Mormon Church, she'd visited several churches in the Chicago area. Drake had found an intellectual and social, if not a spiritual, home in the local Unitarian Church where they had met on an Easter Sunday some two years before.

She thought back twenty years to the months she'd waited for her missionary to return. She had become infatuated, she realized now, with a boy in her high school; at the time she thought it was true love. They had dated, behaved themselves, and had grown more and more to want to be with each other. After graduating from high school, he'd worked for more than a year to earn money for his mission. She wondered now why young men spent two years of their time at their own expense in some of the most godforsaken areas in the world trying to convert third-world citizens to a first-world religion.

But her young man had gone. At her present age, she could see how the misunderstanding had happened. She thought she was waiting for her future husband. He possessed no such feelings and thus felt no commitment to her upon his return as a changed and more mature young man. She, on the other hand, was still emotionally a high school senior. His all-too-soon engagement to one of her older friends (better looking and a snappier dresser) had broken her young heart. That hurt was deep and lasting. If her father had been different, she often thought, he might've helped her recover from what really was an adolescent crush. But he had not been different.

The big turning-point in my life, she recalled, *came when I decided to take some additional computer classes.* She thought about the other twists and turns her forty-one years of life had taken, including some of her sexual dalliances before she left Belnap's employment.

She also remembered how hard her father had worked to provide a good home with all the physical necessities of life. She remembered most, however, his harsh orthodoxy and how literally he'd taken "the Word of God." That "Word of God" included the Bible, literally; the Book of Mormon, literally; the other Mormon scriptures, literally; and every pronouncement of every leader of the Church of Jesus Christ of Latter-day Saints, literally. They were the mouthpieces of the Lord. To ignore their advice was to hazard your eternal salvation. When she pointed out apparent contradictions between what Brother A and Brother B had written on a given topic, her father went into a rage, told her Satan was after her soul.

Good old Mom. She always came to my rescue. In Mom's eyes, Dad was a fanatic, but I could do no wrong.

"Now, Father, you can't expect a nineteen-year-old girl to understand the gospel the way you do. Besides, you have the priesthood and she doesn't. Leave her alone—she'll be all right."

And then Mom would take her into the kitchen, show her the latest fashion magazine, and help her select the pattern for her next dress. Being an only child made Harriet the focus of most of her mother's energies. Anything Harriet wanted, her mother would try to get for her.

One thing she wanted—especially when she was in her twenties—was to move out of her parents' home, to be on her own. Her father harshly opposed the idea, and her mother killed it with her tears.

As she waited in the motel, Harriet thought of the moment when she realized that her mother had spoiled her. *Maybe that's why I thought I could have Grant Belnap, too.* But that was after she had been forced to resign, after her affair with the bishop's counselor, after her excommunication, and after the death of her parents.

CHAPTER NINE

EXCOMMUNICATION

Harriet relived the experiences of her excommunication, experiences still etched in her mind. The letter from the bishop had been characteristically blunt and to the point. She thought at the time that her father would've written just such a letter, had it been his responsibility. The letter stated:

Your bishopric has scheduled a disciplinary council to consider your alleged conduct not consistent with membership in the Church of Jesus Christ of Latter-day Saints. This action could result in your being disfellowshipped or excommunicated.

Please attend this disciplinary council in the bishop's office on Thursday, 11 October 2012, at 8:00 p.m. If this time is not convenient for you, please contact one of the undersigned.

If you are not present and have not made arrangements for a new time, the council will proceed in your absence and a decision made on the basis of the evidence at hand.

The letter, signed by all three members of her bishopric—Bishop Harvey Jones, and his counselors Robert Baker, and Warren Axelson—had been hand-delivered to her by Baker and Axelson. It had not mentioned the fact that she and the bishop had talked at length in his office earlier about those allegations. When confronted, she had confessed her affair frankly to her bishop in the hope that the inevitable disciplinary council would be lenient, but at the same time she had pleaded for her membership in the Church. "If I'm excommunicated, it will kill my mother," she had tragically told her bishop on that earlier occasion. At no time had she mentioned her additional violations of the law of chastity.

She relived her appearance before that council, which she regarded as just one more example of patriarchal control—no women would sit in judgment at her trial. She knew from her reading of church history that disciplinary councils had been called "church courts" for about the first 150 years of the Church's existence. She knew, further, that there had been legal reasons for the name change. The procedure and the possible penalties, however, remained essentially the same.

She had appeared at the time and place, dressed demurely, and had sat in the hall for what seemed an eternity. She didn't know that the three members of the bishopric had knelt in solemn prayer before discussing her case. They asked the Lord to help them know the right steps to take. They desired the wisdom to help save this unfortunate woman from her sins. They told the Lord of their concern for the welfare of her parents, who'd be crushed by her excommunication. They had also told the Lord, as a way of reminding themselves, that the reputation of the Church must be guarded. She didn't know of the deep concern with which these lay leaders of her ward approached their distasteful task or of the genuine love all members of the bishopric felt for each member of the ward. Had she heard their discussion, she would've known she'd receive a fair hearing. However, because she'd heard horror stories of other disciplinary councils not held with the same spirit of compassion and concern, she was more distressed than she needed to be.

Finally, the door to the bishop's office had opened, and the bishop invited her to come in. His counselors rose as she entered.

"Please sit here, Sister Hudson." Bishop Jones indicated a

well-built chair in his plain but adequately furnished office. When all were seated, the bishop addressed her.

"Sister Hudson, my counselors and I have discussed certain aspects of these proceedings, but I've not shared with them what you've told me. May I have your permission to do so now?"

"I'll tell them myself, Bishop. And I appreciate the fact that my confession has been confidential. Yes, brethren, I have committed adultery with a highly placed married man in a neighboring ward. This took place over a period of several months late last year. That's the sum and substance of it." Harriet had felt no need at that point to be coy or evasive.

"Thank you, Sister Hudson," Bishop Jones told her, kindly but sadly. "Brethren, do you have any questions for Sister Hudson?"

Baker asked, "Were there any extenuating circumstances, Sister Hudson? Did this man pursue you? Did he force his attentions upon you? Did he insist on continuing the relationship after you wanted to end it?"

"No, Brother Baker. I was the aggressor in this whole affair. I have a strong sex drive, and I knew the man had a very cold wife. No, I am not a nymphomaniac, but I did take advantage of him for my own desires. He wanted to stop the whole thing after the first encounter, but I kept after him, and we had what the tabloids would call a sensational, if only temporary, affair."

The men blushed at her unexpected frankness.

Axelson cleared his throat before asking, "At the time, did you have any feelings of guilt? Any concerns about the effects of your behavior on this man and his family, or upon you and your wonderful parents?"

"Brother Axelson, I knew what I was doing, and at the time I just didn't give a damn. Now the affair is over, he's been released, shamed, excommunicated, his wife and family have been terribly hurt. Yes, I can see that my behavior was immoral, reckless, and irresponsible. I regret that. But given the same circumstances, I'd probably do it again."

She noted their shocked looks. She stared directly at each of them in turn, and the men uncomfortably dropped their eyes.

"You can give no reasons, then, why we shouldn't proceed in accordance with church standards?" Jones asked.

"Yes, Bishop, I can. The reason is my mother."

"But not your father?"

"I regard my father as a sanctimonious fanatic; if whatever you now do to me hurts him, I'm glad. No, it's my mother I worry about. If I'm excommunicated, it'll kill her. You understand what I'm saying? If you excommunicate me, you'll sentence my mother to death."

They understood what she was saying. After more discussion, Bishop Jones asked her to wait outside while they deliberated.

Unbeknownst to her, they reviewed the facts: the excommunication of her partner in sin; the contributions her parents had made to the ward and the Church; the possible effects of her excommunication upon her parents, particularly her mother, for whom they felt warm affection and concern.

They talked about the scriptural example of the woman brought before the Lord, having been caught in the very act of adultery, and about his statement: "Neither do I condemn thee; go and sin no more." And they talked about a now flamboyantly unrepentant sinner—yet one who had confessed earlier to her bishop. They discussed their duty to protect the reputation of the Church and their duty to help sinners to repent. The bishop asked each counselor for his recommendation, and then announced the decision, which was his alone to make: excommunication. Would his counselors support that verdict? Each nodded. Then, kneeling in prayer, they asked the Lord to confirm their decision.

Although Harriet knew nothing about the details of their deliberation, she wasn't surprised by their verdict when she rejoined them.

Bishop Jones told her softly, "If there had been any semblance of remorse or guilt, any extenuating circumstances, we might've come to a different decision. But given the facts, which you don't dispute, our only recourse is to excommunicate you from the Church of Jesus Christ of Latter-day Saints."

"You have just killed my mother, and for that I will never forgive you." Harriet Hudson stood up and walked out.

CHAPTER TEN

DEATH AND SUICIDE

As she sat in her motel room, Harriet recalled her mother's collapse. Did her already high blood pressure contribute to the stroke? She could still see her completely paralyzed mother in the nursing home, unconscious, breathing on a respirator at her father's insistence. *Why,* she had wondered ever since, *can't we let dead people die? Mom was not alive in that nursing home. Why did my father have her blessed by the elders of the Church? Why had he insisted on those measures that only postponed the inevitable?* Five painful and expensive months passed before this doting, long-suffering woman had died—technically, finally, and officially.

The funeral had been held in the same building as her trial, conducted by the same bishop. The speakers had told of her mother's devotion to the Church, to her husband, and to her daughter. Harriet agreed with that part of the service. Others had praised her father's total devotion and care. Harriet thought those words reeked of hypocrisy. He had been anything but a devoted husband.

And he supplied the proof of that hypocrisy when, only three months later, he married a widow not much older than Harriet herself and the antithesis of Harriet's mother. She had moved into the ward shortly after the excommunication. One of Harriet's friends described her as a suicide blonde—"dyed by her own hand."

Harriet often wondered what really made her father tick. She had never asked her mother why there were no other children. Had her father lived with suppressed and unfulfilled sexual desires all his married life? Was her mother as cold as her own lover's wife? Could this account for her father's harshness, his strictness, his literal interpretation of what membership in the Church meant? She hadn't noticed it when she lived at home, but now she wondered. Harriet felt no sympathy because of these possibilities. Rather, she relished the fact that the marriage had lasted just long enough for this sexy broad to clean out her father's savings account and disappear.

Her father had chosen suicide as his way out. He had driven to the west desert near Wendover, the Nevada gambling city attractive to thousands of Salt Lakers. The police, alerted by hot-rodders on the flats, had found his car and body within a few days. He had shot himself in the head. She hadn't grieved at her father's death. Instead, she hated him all the more. He'd been willing to bring his own suffering to an end but not her mother's.

Shortly after her father's funeral, she sent out resumes to law firms in several cities and accepted an offer from a firm in Chicago. She had not listed Grant Belnap as a reference. Bitterly, she continued to blame the Mormon Church for the deaths of her parents. In Chicago she had started to smoke and drink. She didn't like her job. She was effective and competent, but it was monotonous.

Sherman Drake helped break that monotony. And when he told her about the manuscript as a way to hurt Belnap and his Church, she was very interested. Drake had convinced her that the manuscript would prove the Book of Mormon wasn't translated from golden plates by Joseph Smith but had been written by an unknown person about 1800. Drake had convinced her that experts had tested the paper, the ink, and the handwriting, verifying all Drake claimed. She had agreed with him that the Catholic diocese in Salt Lake would provide the most help in bringing this new revelation to the media.

She'd followed Drake to Salt Lake City under false pretenses. He thought she wanted to be in Salt Lake City to gloat when the story broke. Yes, Harriet had come to Salt Lake for that purpose. But mainly she was there to hurt the Church and Grant Belnap. She was convinced Belnap would do anything to suppress that evidence and had fantasized freely about that "anything"—even marriage!

CHAPTER ELEVEN

SHERMAN DRAKE

Monday, 11 May 2020

After Bishop Donovan led him to the door, Sherman Drake walked back to the secretary's desk, not knowing her boss had just instructed her to make the appointment no earlier than four days.

"Bishop Donavan told me to set up an appointment. I hope it can be soon—like tomorrow or the next day."

"Let me see what his calendar's like. My goodness, he's booked solidly for the next three days. How about four o'clock in the afternoon of Friday, May 15?"

Drake felt his hackles rise. *Doesn't that idiot know how important this is?* But he controlled his temper and responded, "If that's the best you can do, it'll have to do. But please put my name down for any time that opens up before the 15th, okay? I can be reached at my motel." And he gave her the number.

"I'll do that, sir. And your name again, please?"

"Sherman Drake." He smiled unpleasantly. "A name you just might come to remember."

Drake made his way back to his motel, after a long stop for supper and a beer. While eating he mentally rehashed his meeting with the Catholic leader. *He didn't react at all the way I thought he would,* he mused. *He didn't seem excited about what I told him. But he did accept the manuscript. I wonder what he'll do with it? And this business of being too busy to see me for four days bothers me. What's he up to? What's he thinking?* Drake paid his bill and drove back to his motel.

Drake knew the Book of Mormon spoke of the "great and abominable church." He also knew that some early Mormon leaders publicly identified that great and abominable church as the Catholic Church, a view that had been soft-pedaled, even denied, many years since.

Drake had first encountered Mormonism when he became friends with some Mormon fellow students at Berkeley who invited him to attend a social at the LDS Institute of Religion. There he had met Kathy Phelps. Ah, Kathy! What a woman! She was outrageously beautiful, extremely bright, unbelievably talented, and completely stubborn.

It was her physical appearance that hit him first. She was a head-turner. When she walked into a crowded room at the institute, all eyes followed her and conversation momentarily hushed. She had been easy to talk to, easy to become acquainted with, and a delight to be around. After their first meeting, Sherman couldn't get her out of his thoughts.

So he continued to attend functions at the institute, hoping Kathy would be there. Usually she was. More often than not they struck up conversations, usually on innocuous topics such as classes, grades, professors, and letters from home. He held his own with her on all topics except letters from home. She reported all sorts of interesting doings of her large family in southern Idaho, but he had no family.

His mother had raised him without benefit of a husband and had died from an overdose of some weird street drug when he was twelve. He constantly repressed his conviction that she supported the two of them as a prostitute. After she died, until he was eighteen, he lived in a series of foster homes, some bad, some good, especially the last one where his foster-father was a Bay Area physicist. This man encouraged him to get all the education he could so he would "amount to something." His very high SAT score and the recommendation of his foster-father helped him gain admission to Berkeley.

His unremitting desire to be around Kathy led him to attend not only the social functions of the institute, but the religious instruction classes as well. His friends at the institute were eager to have him join the Church. Despite his misgivings he felt drawn in that direction because of his almost uncontrollable desire for Kathy Phelps. He loved her mind. He admired her talents. But most of all, he was almost insane with desire for her body.

When he became convinced that there was no other way to get closer to Kathy, he was baptized. She attended the service, congratulating him warmly. He also felt warmed—but it was the heat of sensual desire. He fantasized that he was going to marry this talented goddess.

His fantasies were shattered the following Sunday where, as was the custom, the bishop read his name to the congregation for the unanimous if perfunctory vote of acceptance into the ward. After the meeting, he scanned the congregation, looking for Kathy. Ah, there she was. Beaming excitedly, she introduced him to her fiancé. "He flew in from Harvard yesterday, and last night he gave me this ring. Isn't it gorgeous?"

It was indeed gorgeous. Sherman's fantasy bubble burst in his face. He muttered something in the nature of congratulations, turned, and left the chapel, never to return.

The name George Stratford had not at any time entered Sherman and Kathy's conversations. He came as a complete stranger to Sherman. But he changed the direction of Sherman's life forever.

It hurt him to remember these events. He tried not to think of the subsequent attempts of his friends at the institute to engage him in its social and religious activities. He dropped out of Berkeley at the end of the term, despite the protestations of his foster-father. Thus the course of his life was altered totally and completely.

He worked at odd jobs, far below his intellectual capacity. He then learned of a group of fundamentalist Christians in the Berkeley area who were focused on debunking the claims of the Mormon Church. While he had no interest in their views on life and religion, he was very interested in learning anything and everything he could that would prove the Mormon Church fraudulent. On the fringes of that group were a few individuals who seemed to share Sherman's hatred of everything Mormon. Mitchell Potter, although descended from early Mormon pioneers, was one of those individuals. And that made all the difference for Sherman.

Mitchell Potter was a dabbler. He explored one area of philosophy, became bored, then turned to another. One of his interests was original historical documents. While Potter continued to pursue different avenues of interest from time to time, he always came back to historical documents. His occasional finds with monetary value in the document market provided money for his food and shelter. But their shared antipathy for Mormonism drew Drake Sherman and Mitchell Potter together.

Within two months, Drake moved into Potter's apartment and developed a keen interest in what Mitch was doing. Mitch's interest in historical documents took him twice to Chicago. After the second trip, he told Drake he was going to move there permanently.

"Want to come along, Sherm?"

Together they moved to the Chicago suburb of Des Plaines. Some of their neighbors at first wondered if they were gay, but the frequency with which women showed up on the premises soon dispelled that notion. Both found jobs to finance their minimal lifestyle. Potter worked in a bookstore where his life-long wide reading made him a valuable asset. Drake was a spotter at a large interstate trucking firm—far from being as intellectually challenging as his life at Berkeley. And both started to attend a local Unitarian Church.

During the coffee hour after the Sunday service on Easter, 2018, Drake met Harriet Hudson. As embittered former Mormons, they struck up an immediate acquaintance. Even though she was about ten years older than Sherman, he found her sensually exciting. Within days, they were having sex in her apartment. Their affair had lasted two years now, and both seemed equally insatiable.

CHAPTER TWELVE

THE MANUSCRIPT

The telephone jangled sharply.

"This is Sherman Drake." He never just answered, "Hello."

"That you, Sherm?" the caller had to ask. "The one and only Sherman Drake?" Harriet Hudson's voice could not be mistaken. "I got in on schedule and came right to the motel. Sorry my work didn't let me fly out with you."

She was soon in his motel room. Over a beer, they recalled the conversation that had brought them to Salt Lake.

"I learned something the other day that just might interest you," Sherman had told her two weeks earlier.

"And what might that be?" she had asked.

"The Book of Mormon is a plagiarized piece of fiction."

"I've known for a long time it was fictional. But plagiarized? What makes you say that?"

"Mitch Potter told me a couple of weeks ago that he had a lead on a document that might prove the Mormon Church fraudulent. I wanted to know all about this document. Where was it? Could we examine it?"

Mitch had told him, " Yeah, this guy I met at a convention told me he has what appears to be the original handwritten Book of Mormon. He claims he's had it checked by experts and they pinpointed the time of its writing at between 1795 and 1805."

Sherman had been incredulous. "What? That's about when Joseph Smith was born. And the Book of Mormon wasn't even published until 1830."

"Yeah, I know," Mitch responded. "So Joseph Smith must

have stolen his story of the ancient Americans from this document. But how'd he get his hands on it? Where has the document been ever since?"

Sherman had almost exploded with excitement. "Do you have any idea what this means? The implications are unbelievable! This could be the end of the Mormon Church! And what effect would debunking Mormonism have on other churches? Would their basic assumptions also be challenged, or would they pick up the pieces and absorb all of the disenchanted Mormons?"

Mitch raised his eyebrows mockingly, "Don't count your exposés before they're unmasked, Sherm. First, I have yet to see this document. Second, I'm sure the guy who has it now has his own agenda for it. I certainly would if it were mine."

Harriet had interrupted Sherman's story to ask excitedly, "Do you think you can get your hands on that document? How long would it take to authenticate it again? Would the experts who authenticated it realize what a damaging document they were examining? Can I work with you on this thing? Together we could bomb Joe Smith's Church back to the nineteenth century!"

"Easy does it, Harriet. One careful step at a time, please. The guy who told Mitch about this thing is something of a jerk. I doubt he's smart enough to realize what he has, if, indeed, he has it. But, as a matter of fact, Mitch was able to bring this document to our apartment last week"

That had been Sherman's opportunity.

"Mitch doesn't know I took the manuscript," he worried. "Hope I can get it back before he misses it."

"Well, are you ever going to tell me how your meeting with the big bishop went today?" Harriet asked.

"Not too bad, except I get the feeling he's stalling me. That bothers me. Why wouldn't he just jump on it?""

"Oh, no!" Harriet exclaimed. "I just remembered! Bishop Donavan and Anthony Ririe went to high school and the University of Utah together. Do you suppose that has anything to do with the stall?"

"Just who is this Anthony Ririe, anyway?" Sherman demanded.

"He's just about the most powerful man in the Mormon Church!"

Sherman was outraged. "Why didn't you tell me this sooner? I could've taken my stuff to Denver or right to the Cardinal in Chicago, or anywhere. I wonder if those two high holies are cooking something up? That was stupid, Harriet. You might've just ruined the whole thing. Why'd I bring you into this in the first place? That was *my* stupidity." He paced nervously as he spoke.

"How close are those two holy bigwigs, anyway?" Sherman demanded.

"Close enough to be life-long friends. They played tennis on the same team in high school and the university. Ririe attended Donavan's installation as bishop. I guess they are closer than any duo made up of one Mormon and one Catholic leader. I'm really sorry, Sherman. I feel like an idiot for not thinking of this before. Must've had something else on my mind."

She had indeed had something else on her mind. She had been determined to hurt Grant Belnap as well as the Mormon Church. The unmasking had to take place in Salt Lake City. Even if she'd remembered the connection between Ririe and Donavan, she might've disregarded the implications for Sherman's—and her own—scheme.

Their evening did not go well from that point on.

CHAPTER THIRTEEN

THE SEARCH

Early Tuesday morning, 12 May 2020, Grant Belnap and Anthony Ririe met in Ririe's office. After reviewing the events of the previous day, Ririe suggested, "Grant, I think it might be wiser for you, rather than for me, to ask for any records we might have on Sherman Drake. Coming from me might make the request look more important. Heaven knows it's important; we just don't want too many others to think so, too."

"It'll be done as soon as the Membership Department opens at eight o'clock. I'll get back to you." So saying, Grant Belnap walked back to his office. When he called the Membership Department at 8:01, he received a cursory, "Hello, Membership Department. How can I help you?"

As soon as Grant Belnap gave his name, the tone on the other end of the line changed markedly. "Yes, Elder Belnap. This is Steve Henderson. In what way may I be of service, sir?"

"Would it be possible for you to come to my office immediately? I prefer not to handle this matter by telephone."

"I'll be there as soon as I tell my supervisor."

"Brother Henderson, I don't want you to tell your supervisor. I want our meeting to be confidential. Can you arrange that?"

"Of course, sir."

When Henderson arrived in Belnap's office, Belnap asked him to look up Sherman Drake, now living somewhere in the Chicago area, and to bring the information to him personally without telling anyone else in his section.

"Elder Belnap, if this Drake is a member of record and

hasn't asked to have his name removed from our files, I should have the information in a very few minutes," Henderson explained earnestly. "If his name has been removed at his request, however, I'll need to get my supervisor's permission to look in the extra-confidential files. That'll take a bit longer."

"If you can't locate his record in the normal way, stop looking and just let me know."

The record-keeping proclivities of the Church of Jesus Christ of Latter-day Saints are legendary. The Church had been on the cutting edge of computer technology for decades. In a very few minutes, Steve Henderson, having eliminated the records of four other Sherman Drakes, walked back to Grant Belnap's office with a copy of the membership record of Sherman Drake, living in Des Plaines, a Chicago suburb. That record, created at Drake's baptism, showed when he had moved to Des Plaines and gave his address as of April, 2019. Also listed were the ward and stake where his present address would place him.

Belnap thanked Henderson, cautioned him again about confidentiality, and called Jared Price, the bishop of the Des Plaines ward.

"This is Grant Belnap in Salt Lake, Bishop. Sorry to have to bother you at your office."

"No problem, Elder Belnap. What's on your mind?"

"Sherman Drake is a member of your ward. What can you tell me about him?"

Bishop Price, with some surprise, explained, "In our Priesthood Executive Committee meeting just this Sunday, our elders' quorum president reported that Sherman Drake is completely bitter about the Church—wants his name removed, although he hasn't made a formal request."

"Has he attended any meetings since arriving in your area? I see by the record that was about two years ago."

"Absolutely none. I learned last Sunday that he threatened his home teachers with violence if they didn't leave immediately. I assume from that exchange he brought his bitterness with him from the Berkeley Institute Ward."

"Does the address I have here agree with your records? It does? Thank you, Bishop Price. Please keep this inquiry confidential, even from your counselors and clerks."

"Whatever you say, Elder Belnap. Is there anything else?"

"That about does it. Thanks again. May the Lord continue to bless you in your calling."

Belnap immediately called the director of the Berkeley Institute at his home because of the time difference.

"Brother Turley, this is Grant Belnap in Salt Lake City. Hope I'm not calling too early."

"Not at all, Elder Belnap. I was just leaving for work."

"Good. You must regard this call as very confidential. Is anyone in the room with you?"

"No, sir. My wife has already left for her day at the Oakland Temple. I'm alone in the house."

"What can you tell me about Sherman Drake?"

Clark Turley knew as much about Drake as anyone in the Bay Area. He'd fellowshipped him as an investigator, performed his baptism, tried to reactivate him, and sorrowed when he left town. He filled Belnap in about his activities, his obvious infatuation with Kathy Phelps, his friendship with Mitchell Potter, and his subsequent move to Illinois. "He's ignored the letters I wrote him after his move. That's about all there is to tell."

"Thank you, Brother Turley. You've been most helpful. Let me again stress that my call is not to be discussed with anyone, and that includes your associates at the institute and your wife."

"I get the message, Elder Belnap, I get the message. Anything else I can do to be helpful?"

"Not at this time, Brother Turley. Good to talk with you. Goodbye." Belnap went to Ririe's office to report his findings.

Ririe summarized, "So, Sherman Drake was hardly dry from the baptism before he became disaffected. But what does that really tell us about him?"

Belnap responded, "Obviously we're dealing with a man who despises the Church."

Just then Beverly Moore called through the intercom. "A bishop from Des Plaines, Illinois, wants to talk with Elder Belnap. Elder Belnap's secretary thought it sounded urgent and transferred the call here. The bishop says he has more information relative to Elder Belnap's earlier call."

Tony Ririe motioned for Belnap to take the call, flipped on the speakerphone, and told Beverly to put the call through.

"Yes, Bishop Price. What do you have?"

"It may not be important, Elder Belnap, but I just remembered that one of our members, a recent arrival from your area, told me that she'd run across Harriet Hudson, whose family she'd known in Salt Lake. During their brief conversation the Hudson woman had mentioned she had a Mormon boyfriend—Sherman Drake."

"Thank you, Bishop," assured Belnap. "You did the right thing in calling me back. Once again, I stress confidentiality is the word. You've been most helpful. Goodbye."

Tony Ririe noted, "So there *is* a connection. But does that information get us anywhere?"

"It may be that Harriet Hudson and Sherman Drake are staying together here in Salt Lake," Belnap responded. "But where? I don't know any of her old friends. Her mother died about six months after Harriet was excommunicated, and her father committed suicide about a year later. So, does that put us any closer to Drake? I think not."

"Grant, we both have meetings for most of the rest of the day. Would you be available around 4:00? We need to keep moving on this thing."

"I'll be in this chair at four o'clock, Tony."

CHAPTER FOURTEEN

MITCHELL POTTER

Just before he left for work that same day—Tuesday, May 12th—Mitch Potter looked for his manuscript without success.

I'm sure I put it right here. Where the hell is it? The manuscript was missing and so was his roommate. Yes, Drake was taking a "quick trip" out west, but he hadn't mentioned anything about taking the manuscript.

Could that idiot have taken the manuscript with him? Mitch wondered.

Then he noticed the note on the refrigerator door: "Mitch, I hope you won't be too mad at me. I've borrowed the manuscript for a couple of days. I guarantee to bring it back in perfect shape before the weekend. Don't try to reach me because I don't know where I'll be staying. See you Sunday or Monday at the very latest."

If I was upset before, now I'm mad as hell, Mitch told himself. He had obtained the manuscript from Albert Trask, a University of Chicago graduate student and friend. He'd promised to have it back by the time Trask returned from a brief jaunt to Washington, D.C. where he'd gone to do some research at the Library of Congress, sources not available through the Internet. Trask had told him that he needed to know more about the origins of the Book of Mormon and of the Mormon Church itself. He hoped his research would shed some light on the manuscript he'd discovered in an old trunk in his grandfather's house, a house that had been in the family since about 1870.

Mitch tried to deduce Sherman's whereabouts. He telephoned Harriet Hudson and heard a message on her answering machine to call back on Monday. *Had Sherm and Harriet Hudson gone somewhere together? Harriet hailed from Salt Lake City and had a Mormon background. Could they have taken the manuscript to Salt Lake? But why?* Mitch was very much aware of Sherman's strong antipathy for anything Mormon. *So why would he take this manuscript into the heart of the enemy's camp?*

Potter had seen a TV docudrama not long before describing a notorious case of forgery and murder in the Salt Lake area in the 1980s. The forgeries were documents dealing with the early history of the Mormons. If any of those involved were still around, they'd give anything to get their hands on the manuscript now in Sherman's possession. So, too, would any of their intellectual heirs, both in and out of the Mormon Church.

So, where does that leave me? And what can I do to track Sherm down and get that document back to Trask as soon as he returns?

He wondered who would profit most from an exposure of the Mormon Church as a fraud—some of the evangelical types?

Then he had another idea, Sherman's phone calls. When he got to work, he called the phone company help line, identified himself as the responsible person for calls charged to his number, and then asked for a list of long-distance phone calls made from his phone in the last week.

Yes, a call had been made to Salt Lake City three days earlier. He called directory assistance in that area code. The number was the Catholic Diocese.

"So he's gone to the Catholics in Salt Lake City with that pesky manuscript," Mitch spoke to an empty room. After he returned from work, he called the same number.

It wasn't easy to get past Bishop Donavan's secretary; but when Potter mentioned Sherman Drake's name, she put him through.

"Your Excellency, my name is Mitchell Potter. I'm Sherman Drake's roommate. I believe he might've contacted you yesterday."

"Yes, he did come to see me yesterday."

"An emergency's come up, and I need to contact him immediately. Do you have any idea where I can call him?

Pat Donavan paused, thinking fast. "I have a local number for him; but since I don't know you, perhaps it would be better if I had him call you."

"That'd be fine with me, sir. I'd appreciate that very much."

"Perhaps I should get your phone number in case I can't reach Mr. Drake."

As Donavan hung up, he mused about this hitherto unknown roommate. *A family emergency? In that case, wouldn't the family call?* He picked up the phone and keyed in Tony Ririe's number.

"Tony, this is Pat. More news for you. Sherman Drake's roommate, Mitchell Potter, just called me from Des Plaines. Wants to get in touch with Drake immediately. Says there's an emergency. I have Drake's telephone number in the Chicago area as well as the number of his motel here in Salt Lake City. I didn't give Potter Drake's number here."

Ririe's voice held a note of excitement. "Pat, I appreciate this information. It'll be most valuable to me. By the way, so far I've told only Grant Belnap and our documents expert about our meeting yesterday, and I've shown Grant the pages I have. We've learned quite a bit about Sherman Drake—a disaffected one-time Mormon. As you told me yesterday, he has no love for anything to do with my church."

Just as they said good-bye, Grant Belnap appeared in Ririe's office. "I trust Beverly told you I wouldn't make it by four. Sorry," Grant apologized.

"No problem. Somehow I managed to keep busy," he responded wryly.

After sharing what he had learned from Bishop Donavan, Ririe asked, "Where does that leave us now, Grant?"

"I've been trying to make some sense out of this whole thing, Tony. Here are some things we must consider. First, what if the document *is* real and proves to be the source of Joseph Smith's original Book of Mormon? Second, if it proves to be a fake, do we need to take any action? Third, what if we are not the ones who prove the document true or false?"

"Slow down, Grant. You left me speechless after your first 'what if.' Of course the document's false. How can it be otherwise?"

Grant leaned back in his chair before answering. "No offense, President, but you think like a CPA; I think like a trial lawyer. My faith tells me the document is false. My training tells me it could be true. I never went to court without more than one way around a given finding of fact. I doubt very much that Robert McDonald can pin down its authenticity, one way or another, given the time constraints. We need to buy more time for him to do his job and for Bishop Donavan's people to do theirs. If we can do that, and after we have determined that it's false, we can have outside experts verify our findings. If— and this is speculation only—we find it to be authentic, we must have a valid, believable, acceptable plan of action ready to limit the damage. Of course, if we can't have more time before Drake demands his manuscript back, others will determine what happens next."

Ririe's face showed his dismay. "This line of reasoning is hard for me to handle, Grant. I'm as certain the Book of Mormon is what Joseph Smith proclaimed it to be as I am of anything in this world. It's unthinkable to me that the man I have revered all my life as the prophet of the restoration was a fraud. Just saying that makes me shudder."

Grant phrased his reply very carefully. "Tony, you've never in your entire life entertained any doubts about the gospel, the

Church, its origin, its organization, or its function, let alone the Book of Mormon. I *have* had doubts, serious doubts, but I resolved them to my satisfaction long ago in a way that permitted me to be active in the Church, to be a part of its leadership at several levels, and to feel the Spirit of the Lord with me in the execution of my duties. As a result, I'm perhaps in a better position than you are to think through this whole matter in a way that'll ensure the best possible resolution. I know it's not diplomatic to make such a statement to my superior officer in the Church; but if we can't be completely honest with each other, we're in worse trouble yet."

Ririe was taken aback. That an apostle should confess to having had anything less than complete faith in the restored gospel, the truth of its origin, the rightness of its mission, and the validity of the Book of Mormon, was hard to take. Nevertheless, he tried to keep the conversation going rather than shut it off. Perhaps there was more he could learn from Grant Belnap and about Grant Belnap himself.

"Grant, I appreciate your candor, although I must say your remarks come as something of a shock." He took a deep breath. "Would you care to share with me some time your journey from your doubts to your present view of the gospel?"

"Tony, my heart, mind, and testimony are open to you. The afternoon is now pretty well shot, but I have the evening free."

"Good, I'm free this evening as well. Could we meet at your house at about eight?"

"My house at eight it is, Tony."

CHAPTER FIFTEEN

PANIC

After talking to Ririe, Bishop Donavan called Drake.

"Mr. Drake, this is Bishop Donavan."

"Bishop Donavan, it's good to hear from you, sir. I was beginning to think you hadn't taken me seriously yesterday."

"That's not why I am calling. I just received a call from your roommate in Des Plaines. I don't know how or why he called me in his attempts to locate you. I didn't give him your local telephone number, but I told him I'd relay his message."

"And that message is?"

"That some sort of emergency has arisen, and he needs to contact you as soon as possible. I hope there hasn't been a death in the family."

"Thank you for handling the call the way you did, sir. I appreciate that. No, I have no family, so the emergency must be something else. Thank you again, sir. I hope we can meet very soon. Are you having some of your experts look at what I left with you?"

"Yes. One of my priests, Father Monahan, has done historical research on the Book of Mormon, and he's going over your manuscript as we speak."

"Good. I'm sure he'll validate my claim that the Mormon Church has a fraudulent base. Is there any chance we can meet before Friday?"

"I'm booked solidly. Besides, Father Monahan will need some time to review the manuscript. Probably more time than we've given him. But, I'll try to see you as soon as possible. Good-bye."

Harriet Hudson had been hovering excitedly over Sherman's shoulder during this conversation. "What was that all about?" she demanded.

"Mitch Potter's trying to reach me. Says it's some kind of emergency. He must've put two and two together and took a chance in calling Bishop Donavan. So he knows I've taken the manuscript."

"Oh! Where does that leave us? Could he put the police on your trail? What're you gonna do?" Harriet could ask questions faster than anyone could answer them.

"Slow down, Harriet. We have to think clearly. I'll bet anything Donavan got in touch with Ririe before he called me. What'll Ririe and his people conclude about Mitch's call?"

"What *can* they conclude?" Harriet wanted to know.

"I don't know. But I'll bet anything Ririe knows a lot about me from church records. I'll bet he knows where I live, where I was baptized, and that I'm a very disaffected nominal Mormon. If those two holy bigwigs are as close as you say, I'll bet Donavan has told Ririe everything—even shown him or given him the manuscript. What Ririe doesn't know is whether the document I left with Bishop Donavan is for real."

"Now it's my turn to bet," Harriet declared. "I'll bet Ririe's certain it's phony. His background and position wouldn't let him think anything else. But would he handle this alone?" Then dismay swept across her face.

"Oh, no, Sherman! I can't believe what I've done. Right after I arrived yesterday, I called one of the leaders of the Mormon Church, Grant Belnap. He turned down my appeal when he was my stake president. He's now one of their Twelve Apostles. I told him it was payback time, and I had the power to blow the lid off his church. He cut me off before I could say more."

"You are a stupid fool, Harriet!" Sherman exploded. "Now

this Grant Belnap'll tell Ririe about your call. And Ririe'll tell him about meeting with Donavan. And this Belnap guy must assume you and I are connected in some way. That really blows it!"

"I need a beer." Harriet took two bottles from Sherman's motel refrigerator. She wanted a cigarette but Sherman was in a no-smoking room, at his request.

Sherman glared at her. "What can you tell me about this Belnap? Will he be as sure as Ririe the manuscript is a phony? Or will his background permit him to think the unthinkable?"

Slowly, Harriett told Sherman, "Grant Belnap is a Harvard man. He's had his spiritual struggles with the faith of his fathers."

"How do you know that?"

"I was his secretary when he was a Salt Lake lawyer. He made me resign when I became infatuated with him."

"Blast you, Harriet! There's a lot about you I don't know, isn't there? You're still after him, aren't you? That's why you came to Salt Lake. Not to be with me, but to try to snare or trap him. You're a devious devil, Harriet."

"No, Sherm. I long since gave up any hope of having Grant Belnap—I just wanted to gloat." Harriet finally faced the end of her fantasy.

Drake tried to maintain his self-control. "Okay, so you know him, and want to gloat. How will he react to the claim of the document?"

Harriet thought for a moment before responding. "Well, his church life wouldn't permit him to entertain the thought of a fraudulent beginning for the Book of Mormon. But his legal mind—and I've seen it first-hand—probably would be looking for ways to limit the damage if he, and the world, were to find out that the foundation of the Mormon Church was fraudulent. That's the way his mind works."

"Harriet, I think this manuscript's in danger," Drake asserted, feeling panicky. "I think our lives are in danger. I think these top Mormons, who know more about the existence of this manuscript and about us than we want them to know, will stop at nothing to protect their precious Church. I'm going to try to get the manuscript back and then we'll take the next flight back to Chicago."

Harriet disagreed. "Aren't you putting it on a little thick, Sherman? These guys don't do things like that." Then she stopped, dismay again filling her eyes. "On the other hand some Mormon leaders were accused of similar things in the early days of the Church. Danites, I think they were called. They policed members who stepped out of line and took care of some troublesome Gentiles as well. They called it blood atonement."

Sherman tried to reach Bishop Donavan by phone but was told he was out of the city until Friday. Father Monahan was also unavailable until Friday.

"Where does that leave us, Harriet? We're stuck in this lousy city for three whole days."

The panic slowly diminished as they spent most of the next three days doing the usual tourist things—Temple Square, reminders of the 2002 Olympics, plays, movies, the cemetery where Harriet's parents were buried, sporting events, the nearby canyons—until their patience and their energies were nearly exhausted.

CHAPTER SIXTEEN

THE RED-EYE

In the meantime, both Robert McDonald and Father Monahan had been hard at work. McDonald tested the paper for indications of age. *If,* he reasoned, *the paper has the qualities of being made in the late 1700s or early 1800s, then the claim of being an old document might have merit. If, on the other hand, it shows signs of much later manufacture, then someone is attempting to deceive. If I had to make a judgment at this point in my investigation, I would say the document looks real. But then I haven't even started to look at provenance.*

Father Monahan, for his part, compared the words, sentence structure, and organization of his part of the manuscript with his reproduction of the first edition of the Book of Mormon.

Both approaches called for meticulous care and patience. Early Thursday morning, each expert contacted his superior and asked for more time. But early Friday morning, Sherman Drake was camped on Bishop Donavan's doorstep. When the first of the bishop's staff unlocked the outer door, Drake went directly to Donavan's secretary just as she walked in.

"I must see Bishop Donavan at once," he demanded.

"I'm sorry, Mr. Drake, but Bishop Donavan hasn't come in yet. Oh, here he comes now." Bishop Donavan was walking down the hall accompanied by a younger priest.

"Isn't that Father Monahan with him?" Drake asked.

"Yes, sir, it is."

"Ah, Mr. Drake," Donavan smiled cheerfully. "As long as

you're here, come in." He nodded to Father Monahan who kept on walking toward his own office.

Once in Donavan's office, Drake demanded, "Sir, I must have my manuscript back at once. I need to return to Chicago at the earliest possible moment, and I can't leave without my manuscript."

"I would like to say, 'Here it is, take it.' But I can't," Bishop Donavan told him. "Father Monahan, whom you saw with me just now, is my resident expert on the Book of Mormon. He's been analyzing the manuscript and has enlisted the help of a colleague. This friend has the manuscript with him at his Ogden monastery but should be back here late this afternoon. I'll call you at your motel the moment he arrives."

Drake wondered if Donavan was telling the truth or was stalling him. "Can't we reach him by phone? I could drive to Ogden and pick it up."

"This monastery has no electronic communication with the outside world, Mr. Drake. I'm afraid you must wait. I'm truly sorry to delay your departure. I hope your need to leave isn't for unhappy reasons."

Drake could hardly contain his fury. "And I hope you're being honest with me, Bishop Donavan. Since we met, I've become aware of your long friendship with Anthony Ririe. I hope you two aren't trying to sand-bag me."

"I'm deeply offended by your remark, Mr. Drake. Perhaps it's time for you to leave. I'll call you as promised."

Angry and frustrated, Sherman Drake stormed out of Donavan's office.

As soon as he was certain Drake was gone, Bishop Donavan called Father Peter Monahan, who, in addition to his other duties, was Bishop Donavan's confessor. "What can you tell me about the document's authenticity, Pete?"

"I'm not getting any closer to the truth, Pat. Based on my

work thus far I would have to say that either this manuscript is a direct copy of the first edition of the Book of Mormon, or"—and he paused—"vice versa."

"I sincerely hope you can prove your first conjecture, Pete, because as much as I disagree with the basic premises of the Mormon Church, I love Tony Ririe more. And most of the Mormons I know are fine people trying to live good Christian lives. But I just lied for Tony Ririe, and I must confess formally to you as soon as I call him about Drake's demand to have his manuscript back."

Donavan called Ririe. "Tony, how is your man doing with his part of the manuscript? Father Monahan needs more time. He's almost at an impasse."

"Maybe the Mormon experts will have to make the final determination," Ririe replied.

"But that isn't the main reason I called," Donavan continued. "Drake was just here and demanded the immediate return of his manuscript. He stormed out of here mad as the devil when I told him the manuscript wouldn't be available until late this afternoon."

"Are you obligated to return the manuscript to Drake this afternoon?"

"Yes, I'm afraid so, Tony. You should get your half to me by four at the latest."

"I'll bring it personally."

At four-thirty on May 15th, Bishop Donavan called Drake. "Your manuscript is now in my office. Come right over if you like, or pick it up in the morning."

"I'll be in your office in less than ten minutes, Bishop Donavan."

After picking up his manuscript, Drake tried to make reservations on the next available flight, but the red-eye leaving at midnight was the first one he could get. He and Harriet then went out for a long supper and some beer. Upon returning to Drake's room, they consumed more beer, then engaged in some brief but unsatisfactory sex before she went back to her own room.

About eleven Sherman picked her up and they headed, albeit unsteadily, to the airport where they returned the rental car, paying the extra drop-off fee. They failed to notice the sedan following not far behind.

On their arrival at O'Hare, about 4 a.m., Saturday, Sherman and Harriet shared a taxi to Des Plaines where she got out in front of her apartment and Sherman went on to his.

Sherman Drake tried to enter his apartment quietly, hoping not to awaken his roommate. Although it was almost five in the morning, Mitch heard the dead-bolt slide back.

"That you, Sherman?"

"Yeah, I'm home."

"Where the hell have you been, and what've you been up to?"

"You know exactly where I've been. Yes, I took the manuscript with me and here it is, exactly as you left it—safe and untouched."

"Good thing for you it is. What in the name of all that's holy were you trying to do in Salt Lake? Sell my document to the Mormons? Sell it to the Catholics?"

Drake tried not to mind being accused of theft.

"Lemme tell you the whole story, Mitch," he purred. "Now, I know it was wrong to take something belonging to you, a trusted friend, without your permission. But let me tell you some things you might not know."

Sherman recounted his meeting with Bishop Donavan, Harriet's surmise that the Mormon leadership had been informed of his visit, and her further guess that Donavan had contacted the Mormons again after Potter's call.

"Now, I'm home. The manuscript's safer here than it would've been in Salt Lake City. Harriet was convinced that both the manuscript and our lives would've been in danger if we'd stayed in Salt Lake any longer. We tried to get an earlier flight but had to settle for the red-eye."

Mitchell blinked at him wearily, only slightly mollified. "Sherman, I have to return that jinxed manuscript to Albert Trask today. You can go with me if you like. Maybe he'll be willing to cooperate with you."

"Yes, I'd like to meet this Trask. Did he ever tell you this manuscript has been authenticated? I told Harriet and Bishop Donavan it had."

"No. I gather he hasn't had time to do that. But it'll need a thorough forensic analysis. If it's a phony, it won't serve your purposes. If it's real, it may be worth a bundle. First, it would be of great interest to a document dealer. Second, it could be sold for even more money to the Mormons so they could suppress it to save their ecclesiastical hides."

Sherman reflected a moment before responding. "Mitch, let's get a few more hours of shut-eye, then call your friend Trask and see when we can get things moving. Okay?"

"Okay. But first let's take a look at the manuscript."

Mitch unfastened the brad on the manila envelope and tipped it forward. Several pages from the *Deseret Tribune* slid out.

CHAPTER SEVENTEEN

BELNAP'S JOURNEY

Tuesday, 12 May 2020

The previous Tuesday evening at eight, Tony Ririe and Grant Belnap met by appointment in the latter's spacious home. After the usual pleasantries at the door, they moved to Belnap's den. Ririe looked again at the two walls of bookcases filled to capacity with books old and new. Ririe correctly assumed that Belnap had read most of them. Belnap motioned Ririe to the larger of two recliners.

"You asked me to share my journey," Belnap began, "but I'd like this to be a conversation, not a monologue."

"I hope I can add something to help make it a conversation," Ririe replied. "But first I must share an additional twist in the whole story, a twist I've been holding to myself for several hours."

Belnap shifted in his chair and leaned forward expectantly.

"As she fixed my unusually early breakfast this morning, Marybeth told me I'd been talking in my sleep about a mysterious document. After a few minutes of back and forth conversation, I gave her the entire account. Now, the question I have for you is, to what extent should I further involve Marybeth in this matter?"Belnap responded without hesitation. "Completely. Not only is she wise but also circumspect. We'll both profit from her input. And you'll feel much more comfortable as you take calls at home about the matter."

"Thanks, Grant. You've reflected my thoughts precisely.

But let's try to put that twist aside for the rest of the evening and get on with our conversation."

"Yes, I've been looking forward to this discussion. Tony, as you know I was raised in the Church by faithful parents. Until I entered Harvard, immediately after my mission to Holland, I was what most people would call a true believer, or what many in the Church call an iron-rodder."

"I remember that term from my university days as well, Grant," Ririe interjected. "It was used during the last century to differentiate between those who interpreted the scriptures quite literally, the iron-rodders, and those who interpreted them somewhat liberally, the liahonas."

"Yes," Belnap continued, "that name comes from the miraculous indicator mentioned in the Book of Mormon, that gave *general* direction. You'll recall that both the liahonas and the iron-rodders were seen as active members who loved the gospel and served in the Church but who possessed different ways of seeing their religious worlds."

"I remember many discussions about those two groups at the University of Utah Institute."

"At any rate, at that time for me, truth was truth and error was error with no middle ground. A straight line divided the two. I knew the gospel was true and could say so on my mission and in testimony meetings. My testimony was fixed, set in concrete, immutable, not subject to change or challenge. But challenged it was."

"Exactly where did that challenge come from, Grant?"

"Well, after my mission I met the outside world in the form of some agnostic, if not atheistic, professors during my undergraduate days at Harvard. It quickly became known I was a Mormon from Utah. From then on it seemed that none of my humanities professors and few of my professors from the so-called hard sciences had anything good to say about religion, particularly a revealed religion such as Mormonism. My astronomy professor, however, was active in one of the main-line Christian churches and my geology professor was an Orthodox Jew. They presented no challenge to my faith and stuck to the known facts of geology and astronomy."

"That doesn't sound too challenging yet, Grant."

"That was just the wind-up. Here's the pitch. My psychology and sociology instructors took every opportunity to challenge religious beliefs of any kind, saying such beliefs consisted of wishful thinking based on myths and a lack of crit-ical thinking. My psychology professor, in particular, made quite a point about measuring facts. He would say, 'If a thing exists, it exists in some quantity. If it exists in some quantity, it's measurable. If you can't measure it, it probably doesn't exist.' I'm not sure he said *probably*; maybe it was *certainly*. "

"I had a psych prof at the U who pushed that line," Tony interjected. "But sorry, I interrupted you."

Grant continued, "At any rate I asked myself how I would measure love of God, God's love for us, or faith, hope, and charity. Did they cease to exist if I couldn't measure them? My straight line between truth and error began to show elliptical indentations."

"I think I understand," Tony said.

"My astronomy course gave me a much different view of the universe than I'd possessed earlier. The very magnitude of the known universe was overwhelming, and the size of what most certainly must lie beyond the limits of our known universe was even more staggering. The age of the earth, as asserted by geol-ogists, challenged my conception of the Bible's declaration that God created the earth in six days or even six thousand years. I came to realize that the Bible was not a handbook of geology. And those elliptical indentations became even more pronounced."

"So, you really felt challenged?"

"Yes, I did. Some of my classmates asked if I really believed the whale swallowed Jonah. 'If you believe the whale swallowed Jonah, you can swallow anything,' they would say derisively."

"How did you handle those challenges?"

"For the most part, I just ignored them. But during my struggles I had an interesting conversation with one of my psychology professors—an avowed atheist who had been a devout Seventh-day Adventist. I once told him, 'You don't believe in life after death; I do. If you're right, after you die you won't have the satisfaction of knowing you were right. If I'm right, I'll have that satisfaction; but if I'm wrong, I'll never know.'"

"An interesting jab. But wasn't that a rather bold thing to say?"

"He took it with a wry smile and called my attention to what he called Pascal's Wager. Pascal—a seventeenth-century mathematician and philosopher—argued that, if God does not exist, the skeptic has nothing to lose by believing in God; but if God does exist, the skeptic could gain eternal life by believing in Him. An interesting concept, but both arguments—mine and Pascal's—sounded like a gambler hedging his bets."

"You weren't willing to believe, just in case, right?"

"Right. Fortunately, there was an LDS Institute of Religion associated with the several universities in the area surrounding Harvard. The director, Harold Bartholomew, was a seasoned veteran of the wars I was facing. Well, Bartholomew suggested I read the novels of Chaim Potok, an ordained Jewish rabbi and one of the most skilled and insightful writers of the last century. The most helpful of Potok's novels was *In the Beginning*."

Belnap glanced up at the bookshelf. "I still have my copy.

David Lurie, the central character, was a brilliant young rabbinical student with more questions than answers. Lurie was not satisfied with the explanations of the faith of his fathers as found in the Talmud. On his own and quite contrary to what was expected, or even permitted, of a rabbi-in-embryo, he had been studying other commentaries written in some instances by those who no longer kept the commandments and, in other instances, even by goyim."

"Goyim?"

"Gentiles. His teacher, Rav Tuvya Sharfman, the man who must approve him for ordination, was considered the greatest authority on the Talmud in the Orthodox Jewish world. In that world, excellence in Talmud was considered the highest of human achievements. Lurie feared that Rav Sharfman would discover his independent intellectual quest and deny him ordination."

Belnap stood up to pull the book off the shelf. "Let me read a few lines. Lurie and Sharfman are engaged in a walking conversation; Lurie is speaking."

He asked me if I would stay on for ordination. I told him I would.

"I will give you your test any time you are prepared."

"The Rebbe will give me ordination despite what I told him?" I ventured the question that had been on my mind through much of the night.

We had stopped at a corner to let cars pass. He turned to me contemptuously. "I will not investigate your ritualistic fringes, Lurie. That is between you and your obligations to the past. Are you telling me you will not be an observer of the commandments?"

"I am not telling the Rebbe that."

"What are you telling me?"

"I will go wherever the truth leads me. It is secular schol-

arship, Rebbe; it is not the scholarship of tradition. In secular scholarship there are no boundaries and no permanently fixed views."

"Lurie, if the Torah cannot go out into your world of scholarship and return stronger, then we are all fools and charlatans. I have faith in the Torah, I am not afraid of truth."

Ririe interrupted to say, "My kind of guy, this Rav Sharfman."

"He struck a responsive chord in my mind and spirit, too. Let me read a few more sentences."

We crossed the avenue and entered the school together. The entrance hall was deserted. He turned to me. I felt his eyes move across my face. He said to me in Yiddish, his voice rasping, "I am not bothered by questions of truth. I want to know if the religious world-view has any meaning today. Bring yourself back an answer to that, Lurie. Take apart the Bible and see if it is something more today than the Iliad or the Odyssey. Bring yourself back that answer, Lurie. Do not bring yourself back shallowness."

Belnap slowly put the book down as Ririe noted, "Powerful stuff, Grant."

"Recommended reading, Tony. But can you imagine my response to that kind of challenge? I could examine my beliefs from any angle I chose! And I'd found several other students at the institute also deeply involved in the same taxing struggle."

"Yes, students have that struggle, especially graduate students in the liberal arts and the humanities. But, then what?"

"At about the same time, I considered again the concept of homeostasis—the physical or psychological equivalent of 'nature abhors a vacuum.' It's a natural tendency toward equilibrium or balance. When we're hungry, we look for food. My mental and spiritual homeostasis expressed itself in a desire to have my childhood spiritual convictions stand in harmony with the new truths I was learning at the university. I didn't want to keep my spiritual beliefs in logic-tight compartments, separated from my awareness of other truths. The imbalance I felt expressed itself in questions about the difference between the biblical time-table of creation and that of the sciences."

"Well, such questions are not too hard to answer, are they?"

"True, but there were more complex questions that perplexed and puzzled me, ate away at my sense of oneness."

"That must have been a tough time for you, Grant."

"It got tougher. In my attempts to restore balance, to create an intellectual unity, I came to demand that my religious beliefs be capable of the same kinds of proof that seemed to accompany the assertions of my teachers and texts."

"So where'd that leave you?"

"At one point before I graduated from Harvard, I even considered leaving the Church. One thing kept me back. It would have been more painful to leave than to stay—painful not only to me but also to my wife, my parents, my family, and to my converts in the mission field. I decided to endure the lesser pain."

The ringing telephone interrupted their conversation. Lifting the receiver Belnap answered, "This is Grant Belnap."

CHAPTER EIGHTEEN

THE SANCTIMONIOUS S.O.B.

"And this is Harriet Hudson. Why haven't you called me back like you promised?" Her words were slurred

Belnap clicked on the speakerphone so Ririe could hear the conversation.

"I'll call you when I think there's a necessity."

"Listen, you sanctimonious s.o.b., I have the power to . . ." Belnap broke the connection.

"We know what she was going to say next," he growled, his distaste visible. "And obviously she's been drinking. I don't care to carry on a conversation with a drunk, even if I know and otherwise like him or her. And I do not like this Harriet Hudson. I sense the influence of Satan when I hear her voice."

Belnap rose from his chair and paced the room. "Tony, could we continue this journey another time? That woman's call has upset my train of thought. I want to be on track when I finish what I have to say."

"I understand, Grant," Ririe responded sympathetically. "And I don't like to hear an apostle of the Lord called an s.o.b."

"I was called that more than once in my law practice. I'm used to it, but *sanctimonious*? That hurts." Belnap said as he attempted to lighten the mood.

"I believe my thoughts would be confused as well if we continued now," Ririe responded. "Harriet Hudson's call upsets me almost as much as Marybeth hearing what I said in my sleep and my letting her in on the whole thing. But let's try to get a good night's sleep. You're a great man, Grant. I've enjoyed hearing you retrace part of your journey, and I look forward to hearing more."

They started for the door but were again interrupted by the telephone.

"This is Grant Belnap."

"Elder Belnap, this is Steve Henderson. I'm the clerk in the Membership Department who gave you the information on Sherman Drake earlier today."

Belnap again switched on the speakerphone. "Yes, Brother Henderson. You sound worried. What is it?"

"I've been debating with myself all day about whether to tell you about this. Not long after I delivered the data on Drake to you, I received another request for the same information from the head of Church Security, Brother Garth Garrick. He asked that I keep his request strictly confidential. He also asked for information about a lady named Harriet Hudson. Elder Belnap, have I done the right thing in telling you this?"

Tony Ririe sank back into his chair. Belnap paced.

"You did exactly the right thing, Brother Henderson. Did Brother Garrick say why he wanted to know about Sherman Drake?"

"No he didn't. And I didn't tell him you'd asked about the same man."

"I'm glad you didn't tell him, Brother Henderson. Now, try not to worry about this. Get a good night's rest. And—this is important—tell no one about Brother Garrick's request and about calling me."

"Thank you, Elder Belnap. I know I won't rest well tonight, but be assured I'll tell no one."

Ririe was the first to speak. "At the risk of sounding trite, I would say the plot thickens."

"It not only thickens, it becomes an inside story. How did Garth Garrick learn anything about Sherman Drake?"

They were quiet for a moment, their minds racing.

"Grant, yesterday you told me . . ."

Belnap put his finger to his lips and motioned toward the rear of the house. The two men walked out to the rear deck where they could not be seen from the street and presumably were away from any hidden mikes. Had they gone to the front, they might have noticed an older sedan parked two houses away where its driver had trained high-powered field glasses on the Belnap home.

Outside, Belnap asked softly, "You were saying, Tony?"

Ririe also spoke in hushed tones, "You told me your house had been checked for bugs last week. Who did it?"

"One of Garrick's men. Is it possible that, instead of checking for bugs, he installed one?"

"And do you suppose my office or my house is bugged, too?" Ririe asked.

"Garrick could have heard the name of Sherman Drake from either source," Belnap reasoned. "But he didn't act on it until after we talked yesterday afternoon. If Garrick has been listening in this evening, he knows that Marybeth knows, but I'm not sure that has any special significance. And, yes, I think your office phone's been tapped, Tony."

"Great Scott! This is hard to believe!" Ririe exclaimed in a harsh whisper. "Is Garrick acting on his own or at someone's direction? If he's being directed, by whom? It has to be someone above him. To whom does he answer among the Brethren? A committee on Church Security? Who's on that committee? We have some homework to do first thing in the morning. Maybe we have a real s.o.b."

They talked for a few minutes, then went to the front porch.

They looked over the city lights from the vantage point of Belnap's hillside home and reflected on how the desert of nearly two centuries earlier had come to blossom as the rose. And now, apparently, there were some new weeds among the roses.

CHAPTER NINETEEN

CHURCH SECURITY

Neither Anthony Ririe nor Grant Belnap slept well that night. Marybeth knew that Tony was still very troubled about the manuscript but she tried to maintain a normal routine through breakfast and his unusually early departure. Grant Belnap was glad his late wife was spared seeing his concern. He was glad, that is, until he wondered how much those on the other side could know about what's going on in the lives of their still-living spouses.

Wednesday, 13 May 2020

Both men arrived at their offices at 47 East South Temple shortly after 6 a.m. After meeting briefly in Ririe's office, they decided to take a drive in Belnap's car while they talked. Belnap turned right on State Street and headed south. This time, Ririe noticed the nondescript sedan after a few blocks.

"Grant, do you still have keys to your old law offices?"

"Yes, the firm gave me the use of a small office where I can take care of my family's legal and business affairs from time to time."

"Good. I think we're being followed. Why don't we sit in one of your conference rooms while we try to figure this thing out?"

Belnap cut over to Main Street and headed north to Second South. His old office was in the Utah One Center.

Soon, two very powerful men were talking in what they hoped would be absolute privacy.

"When we get back to our own offices, Grant, I'd like you to check the reporting line of Garth Garrick. If he reports to one of our innumerable committees, find out who's on that committee."

"Wouldn't that be the Church Security Committee, chaired by Ed Hayes?" Belnap was referring to Edward Hayes, acting President of the Quorum of the Twelve and second in line of succession to the presidency.

"I should've remembered that. Could you find out who else is on that committee? I can't imagine that a former FBI man would be eavesdropping on his own. I have a hunch one of the members of that committee may have put him up to it."

"Don't you really mean you think Ed Hayes is the instigator of all this surreptitious surveillance?" Grant asked.

"Yes, I suppose that's what I really mean," Tony said.

"And if he is, what are you going to do?"

"What would you do if you were in my place?" Tony asked.

"I'd go after him with everything in my power."

"And what power do I have to do anything to him or about him unilaterally? I doubt that he's behind Garrick's activities. But if he proposed or ordered or agreed to the eavesdropping and if he's using information from such surveillance for whatever purposes, doesn't that merit some form of discipline?"

"Yes, it certainly does—but not unilateral discipline—not by you alone," Belnap responded. "At the least he should be sent to preside over a mission in, say, Siberia—with the full knowledge of the Twelve, of course. At the most he should be brought to trial before the entire Twelve."

"I know you're joking about Siberia, and such a trial, as you know, would be devastating. But we'll come to that issue later. I think we need to confront Garrick first. And soon."

"President Ririe, I agree. I think you should call him to your office the moment we get back. I recommend further that you not confront him alone. If you like, I'd be willing to sit in."

Ririe noticed that Belnap had reverted to the formal title. He responded in kind.

"Yes, Elder Belnap. I'll be glad of your counsel."

With that they drove back to church headquarters.

"By the way," commented Ririe, "with Hank Cannon out of town, I won't be involved in a meeting of the First Presidency at eight this morning. That gives us some much-needed additional time. Grant, when we get back I'll call Garth Garrick to my office. At the same time, please find out who else is on that committee, and then come to my office as soon as possible."

When Ririe called the twenty-four-hour Church Security line, the operator who answered told him, "Brother Garrick has been in this morning, President, but left about thirty or forty minutes ago. Oh, here he comes now. I'll put him on."

CHAPTER TWENTY

CONFRONTATION

Odd, wasn't it, that Garrick's absence coincided with ours, Ririe thought. He spoke crisply: "Brother Garrick, this is Anthony Ririe. Would it be convenient for you to come to my office immediately? There's a matter of grave concern I need to discuss with you."

"Yes, of course, President. Should I bring anything with me?"

"Just you and your memory, Brother Garrick."

Grant Belnap had just enough time to give Tony Ririe the names of the other committee members before Garth Garrick appeared.

"Please sit here, Brother Garrick. I'll get right to the point. I have reason to believe you have tapped my office phone and have bugged the home of Elder Belnap, here. Am I right or wrong?"

"President Ririe, I'm totally amazed and extremely offended by these accusations. I deny them completely."

Grant Belnap cleared his throat. "May I ask a question or two, President?"

"Certainly."

"Yesterday, did you ask the Membership Department for the record of one Sherman Drake?" Belnap asked.

"Yes, Elder Belnap, I did."

Belnap continued. "For what purpose did you request that information?"

Belnap and Ririe noticed Garrick's eyes dart around the room, as if seeking a way out of the trap. Garrick took a deep, wavering breath, his words coming rapidly, "Brethren, let me tell you the whole story. First, permit me to retract my unwise denial of your accusations. I ask for your understanding and forgiveness as I give you the facts."

Aha! Belnap thought. *He's throwing himself on the mercy of the court!*

Garrick moistened his lips. "I requested the information on Sherman Drake because I looked on him as a potential threat."

"Why did you think he was a potential threat?"

"Well, because of the circumstances under which he arrived in Salt Lake City." Garrick's mouth hung ajar as he realized he had just made another mistake.

"How did you know he was in Salt Lake?" asked Belnap relentlessly.

"Because I heard you two discuss him."

Belnap saw beads of sweat shine on Garrick's forehead.

"And where'd you hear us do that?"

"Listening to the bug in your home, Elder Belnap, while I was seated in my car about two doors down the street from you. The bug we have in your home is very sophisticated. I can hear conversations in almost any part of the house."

"I see," noted Belnap ironically. "Nothing but the best is good enough for Church Security. And why was this sophisticated bug in my home?"

"Because I felt you were at risk as well."

"From Sherman Drake?"

"Yes, and—uh—from Harriet Hudson."

"And you knew about Harriet Hudson because you'd bugged my home?" Belnap maintained his composure with some difficulty.

"I'm afraid you're right, Elder Belnap."

"But you'd already positioned the bug before Harriet Hudson called me the day before yesterday. Isn't that correct?"

"Yes, sir. The bug was placed last Tuesday."

"And the bug on President Ririe's phone. Why is it there?"

Garrick turned appealingly toward Ririe, almost gabbling out his explanation. "As you know, President Ririe, you have consistently refused to have a Church Security driver. What you may not know is that I've been placed under heavy pressure to guarantee your safety in every manner possible, despite your refusal to cooperate. That's why it's necessary for me to know when you are leaving the building so I—uh—can have someone follow you. Again, I stress that's for your safety. That's why I've had someone monitor your calls—so I could anticipate your comings and goings and have someone look out for you."

Belnap interposed, "From whom do you feel this tremendous pressure?"

"Every time I report to the Church Security Committee, I'm asked if the First Presidency and the Twelve are being fully protected from the irrational actions of those who might wish them harm." Garrick was almost whining.

"Is that questioning coming from all members of the committee or does it arise from one or two in particular?"

"Mainly from Elder Hayes," Garrick muttered.

Neither Ririe nor Belnap was surprised by that answer. They were all too aware of Hayes's almost paranoid concerns and deplored his unwise attempts to involve the Church in one of his favorite right-wing groups. He often asserted that the leaders of the Church were in more physical danger than they realized. There was a conspiracy out there whose sole purpose was to discredit the Church in any way possible. When pressed, however, he was not able to give many details. He had little credibility on that point with the other General Authorities.

Belnap's lip curled. "So you think it necessary to have one of your men follow President Ririe each time he leaves the office. Correct?"

"Elder Belnap, when you have been in law enforcement as long as I have, you constantly look over your shoulder. Since President Ririe won't let us guard him in our usual way, we feel strongly we must guard him however we can."

"Who are 'we'?" Ririe asked.

"Well, I guess I should have said 'I,' since it was my decision."

"To what extent have you involved other members of the Church Security Committee in your decision to tail President Ririe and to bug his phone and my home?" Grant Belnap once more felt the exhilaration he'd experienced as a defense lawyer with a prosecution witness on the stand. He reminded himself, however, that this man wasn't on trial and wasn't under formal oath.

"Most of the time I get input from the Church Security Committee at its monthly meetings. However, few of the committee members are aware of the kinds of surveillance we've just been talking about. At our own weekly staff meetings, we simply go over our assignments except for the times Elder Hayes happens to pop in."

Garrick was speaking more freely now, eager to shift the blame by showing himself the obedient servant. "He usually comes in about the time we're ready to adjourn and says a few words to all present about how important our work is." Garrick paused, then added with feigned reluctance, "Then he waits until everyone has left and follows me to my office."

"For some private words? Perhaps words of instruction? Would it be too strong to say that he gives you orders at such times?" Grant Belnap, despite his distaste, did not pass up the cue Garrick was offering. "So the 'we' you mentioned a moment ago refers to you and to Elder Hayes, correct?"

With great relief, Garrick nodded. "Brethren, I might as well tell you that most, if not all, of the bugging and tailing I've done was at the insistence of Elder Hayes."

President Ririe had been sitting quietly, admiring Grant Belnap's skills and watching Garrick squirm. At this point he interjected harshly, "Are you trying to shift the blame onto a man who is sustained and admired as an apostle of the Lord Jesus Christ? A man who has rendered tireless and magnificent service in his calling for many years?"

But Garrick did not wilt. "President Ririe, I'm an experienced lawman, and I'm willing to face up to my responsibility in this entire matter. But I think it's imperative that you know Elder Hayes's role here. For example, he ordered me to place the bug in Elder Belnap's home."

Belnap, repelled almost as much by Garrick's manner as by his words, asked, "Did he tell you why he wanted to invade my privacy in this way?"

Garrick dropped his eyes and moistened his lips. His voice became whining again. "I hate to tell you this, but it must all come out. And you brethren must take some kind of action. He told me he was concerned about the possibility of your being harassed by scheming females."

"Is that what he really said, or did he say he thought I might be entertaining women in my home?"

"You're right again, Elder Belnap. He told me he had worried about you doing something foolish ever since your wife died. In my opinion, he's a loose cannon on deck, a threat to the well-being of the Church."

Tony Ririe was surprised at Garrick's boldness. "Brother Garrick, do you think he's a threat to the well-being of the Church on the basis of his ordering the bug in Elder Belnap's home?"

"Not that alone, brethren. He wanted me to steal Sherman Drake's document."

"How did he know about the document?" Ririe was incredulous.

Garrick cleared his throat, stalling for time. "I told him about it. And he didn't just ask me to steal it—he ordered me to."

"Did you question that order?"

"I did, President, in the strongest terms," Garrick responded. "I told him I thought such a decision should come only from the First Presidency."

"And what was his reaction to that?"

"He claimed that President Wood wasn't functioning in his position, that he was non compos mentis. He told me President Lund wasn't much better than President Wood. And he told me that the counselors in the First Presidency were junior to him in terms of seniority in the Twelve and that gave him the highest authority to order me to steal the document."

"What did you say?

"I told him I did not want to commit a felony—" Garrick's voice held a note of injured virtue—"even if ordered by a high official in the Church."

Ririe paused for a moment before reacting. "And his response?"

"He reminded me of the slaying of Laban by Nephi at the direction of the Lord so that the records in Laban's possession could go with Lehi and his people. He quoted from the fourth Chapter of First Nephi: 'It is better that one man should perish than that a nation should dwindle and perish in unbelief.' He claimed that what he was asking of me was analogous to what the Lord directed Nephi to do. And then he ordered, 'Do it, or I'll have someone who recognizes my authority do it,' and he left the room. I sat for a while, trying to figure out why Elder Hayes was reacting the way he was; I just didn't know what to make of it."

Elder Belnap was quick with his analysis. "I know what to make of it. It tells me that Elder Hayes thought the document could very well be genuine and, if so, could do irreparable harm to the Church."

But Ririe was more disturbed by another thread in the fabric. "Brother Garrick, who would Elder Hayes be referring to as more willing to do the dirty work?"

"My best guess would be Orvin Collins, my second in command. I have reason to believe he covets my position," Garrick replied.

"Why do you think that, Brother Garrick?" Ririe asked.

"Because of the way he acts when he's around Elder Hayes."

Grant Belnap took up the questioning again. "So, you plan to steal the document as soon as Drake gets it back and presumably deliver it to Elder Hayes. Is that right?"

Garrick again seemed to stall for time to collect his thoughts. "No, Elder Belnap, I will continue to refuse his order even if it costs me my job, which I need badly, because I'm helping my widowed oldest sister with her medical bills."

Ririe and Belnap looked at each other with raised eyebrows.

Then Ririe asked, "Is this conversation being recorded as we speak?"

"Yes, sir, it is," Garrick stated without hesitation.

Ririe got up and motioned for Belnap and Garrick to follow him. They walked past the outer office, through the massive office door, turned left, and exited from the building through the even more imposing double plate-glass door. They stood for a few minutes at the top of the fifteen steps while Ririe gave some specific instructions.

When Ririe, Belnap, and Garrick finished their brief conversation, they went directly to Belnap's office, which, Garrick had assured them, was not bugged. Belnap paused beside his secretary who was visibly startled to see the three of them together. "Norma, please hold all calls from anyone except President Ririe's secretary. We'll be in conference for some time."

Her eyes were curious, but, in the manner of all dedicated personal secretaries, she simply agreed. "Of course, Elder Belnap."

Inside Belnap's office, Ririe spoke first. "We need to learn Elder Hayes's schedule for this weekend without alerting him. Any ideas, either of you?"

"Yes, President Ririe," Garrick responded. "I have his schedule here." He pulled a folded sheet of paper from his inner coat pocket. "He left by air for New York this morning at nine to spend a few days with his son and family in Manhattan. He'll go to church with them on Sunday, and then on Monday attend a board meeting of the insurance company he used to represent. He's serving as a consultant. Should be back in Salt Lake City by early Monday evening."

"Good information, Brother Garrick. I'm surprised he's consulting without my knowing it. Well, there're several things about Elder Hayes I didn't know."

Grant Belnap spoke up. "Brother Garrick, that document won't be back in Drake's hands before Friday, the 15th, at the earliest, while Elder Hayes won't return until the 18th. If he wants someone else to steal it, would he have issued that order before he left for New York?"

"I think that's a distinct possibility."

Their meeting broke up after a few minutes, but not before Ririe ordered Garrick to remove the tap in his office and the bug in Belnap's home. Garrick left immediately to carry out that order.

"Before you leave, Tony," Belnap remarked grimly, "I have to say, as an old trial lawyer, that something bothers me about the way Garrick gave his account of Ed Hayes's involvement in all this." Ririe nodded his agreement.

CHAPTER TWENTY-ONE

HALF A LOAF

Saturday, 16 May 2020, 4:30 a.m.

Sherman Drake and Mitchell Potter, both exhausted because of the hour, stared at the newspapers in Drake's hand, refusing to believe what they were seeing.

Potter was the first to react. "What's going on here, Sherman? Are you trying to pull a switch?"

"I swear that manuscript never left my briefcase while I had it."

"So, where is it now?"

"How should I know?"

"Did you ever walk away and leave it in your car or in your room?"

"That's got to be it! Harriet and I went out to supper when we couldn't get an earlier plane out. I'll bet those thieving Mormons stole it while we were out!"

Sherman then invoked a string of oaths impugning the legitimacy of the thief and clearly stating where he wished that thief—and all Mormons—would go. When his emotions were spent, he turned to Potter.

"Mitch, I know the loss of this manuscript could hurt you and possibly cost you plenty. I'll do all in my power to bear that burden for you or with you. But you gotta know this loss hurts me, too. I had visions of really smashing the Mormons."

"Yeah," Potter responded derisively, "and Joe Smith had visions too. But let me tell you, not all's lost from your point of view. You took only about a third of what Trask has. He wouldn't let the whole thing out of his hands."

"So, I'm not the only sneaky one!"

"But if the part Trask still has is genuine," Potter continued, "you've cut its dollar value by a bundle. He could sue the pants off both of us. On the other hand, if it's for real, you can still accomplish your purpose. You follow me?"

"Every step of the way, Mitch. What should we do next? Or is it a matter of 'we' at this time?"

"You better believe it's a matter of 'we,' because I don't intend to face Trask alone. Let's have a good stiff drink and try to get some sleep. Better still, while I pour, report the robbery to the Salt Lake Police, you sneaky . . ." He started to say, "You sneaky bastard," but stopped short.

Drake was soon on the phone to the Salt Lake City police, talking with the desk sergeant, Harold Sorensen. Sorensen got all the details—name of caller, motel name and room number, possible time of theft, when discovered, and the nature of what was stolen.

"What is the value of the missing manuscript?" Sorensen asked.

"Priceless, absolutely priceless. And I think I know who stole it. It's gotta be someone high in the Mormon Church."

"Why do you say that, Mr. Drake?"

"I have my reasons."

"We'll look into it immediately, Mr. Drake. But your saying that the Mormon Church has something to do with this alleged theft doesn't give me anything specific to go on."

"Just do the best you can, Sergeant. Just do the best you can. I hope to hear from you soon."

Harold Sorensen was a devout Mormon. Although he couldn't believe what he'd just heard, he knew he had to act on it. He dispatched one of his men to the motel to look for evidence of forced entry and to learn anything else he could. Then he called Garth Garrick—with whom he had worked on

Church Security matters many times—at his home, woke him from a sound sleep, and told him all he had learned in that call from Des Plaines.

"What time does your shift end, Harold?" Garrick asked.

"At six."

"I'll meet you as you come off shift, Harold. We need to talk."

Meet they did, and talk they did. What Sorensen learned from Garrick shocked and surprised him. Garrick told him in strictest confidence that he thought his second in command, Orvin Collins, also a former FBI agent, may have stolen the manuscript. He told Sorensen about Elder Hayes's order to steal it and his statement that he would get it with or without Garrick's help. Garrick also told Sorensen he thought that Collins coveted Garrick's top position.

Sorensen was less interested in the politics than the question of what Collins might have done with the stolen manuscript, if, indeed, he had stolen it.

"I rather suspect he'll give it to Elder Hayes at the earliest possible moment."

"So the manuscript could be in Collins's hands until Hayes returns from the East?"

"That would be my best guess. And I guess I should report this new development to President Ririe."

Garrick called President Ririe's home at 8 a.m., apologized for calling him at home on a Saturday, and asked to see him personally to convey an important new development he preferred not to handle by phone.

"Come to the house, Brother Garrick. Maybe Marybeth can fix you some breakfast."

When Garrick told President Ririe about his conversation with Sorensen, Ririe asked, "Why do you think Brother Collins is involved?"

"Because of what Elder Hayes told me about getting someone else to steal it and because of my feeling that Collins is after my job."

"That's interesting, but isn't that in the realm of conjecture?"

"Yes, I suppose it is, President."

"At any rate, that manuscript must not be turned over to Elder Hayes! How can we prevent that?"

Before Garrick could respond, his cell phone rang. Ririe heard Garrick say, "Oh, no! That's terrible! I'll leave for the hospital at once."

Garrick explained to the perplexed Ririe that Orvin Collins had been in an auto accident late Friday evening and was in critical condition at the LDS Hospital.

"Yes, go at once to the hospital and do what you can for Brother Collins and his family," President Ririe ordered, "Let me know how Brother Collins is doing. But as soon as possible find out where his car was taken so you can check it for the manuscript."

When Garrick got to the hospital, he learned that Collins had just died from his injuries. After doing what he could for Collins's wife and family, he called Sorensen and enlisted his aid in locating the car. Sorensen reported to Garrick within the hour that there were no signs of anything resembling a manuscript in what was left of the church car Collins had been driving.

Sorensen was among the mourners at Collins's funeral a few days later where Collins was praised as a faithful Latter-day Saint with a strong sense of morals and ethics. *Could the man just described have stolen the manuscript?* Sorensen tried to learn what Collins might have been doing during the time the document most likely disappeared from the motel and learned that Collins probably had spent most of that evening doing his home teaching. Sorensen smelled a rat. *Why had Garrick so positively identified Collins as Hayes's puppet? And was Collins's fatal accident—so convenient for Garrick— really accidental?*

CHAPTER TWENTY-TWO

YES, BUT

Saturday, 16 May 2020

The stiff drink Potter suggested had turned into several. Potter was awakened by a call from his boss, who wanted to know why, at 10:30 a.m., Mitch hadn't shown up for work, but immediately found the answer to his question in Potter's words—slurred, somewhat incoherent.

"If you're not here on the job, cold sober, by one o'clock, you're fired!"

This, from an otherwise friendly and helpful boss, brought Potter to complete wakefulness. He made some coffee, drank a big cupful, showered, drank more coffee, and headed for work.

Back in his office after attending an early Saturday Mass, Bishop Donavan weighed his options and obligations. *Should I have rejected rather than accepted the document when it was offered? Would it be wise now to call Sherman Drake, if he's still in town, and ask some questions about the document I should've asked earlier?* After considering that option for a few minutes, he telephoned Drake's motel, only to hear, "He checked out late last night."

Three hours later, Sherman Drake roused himself just soon enough to make it to the bathroom before he threw up. While he was cursing hard liquor and cursing himself for not remembering how it sometimes affected him, the events of the previous twenty-four hours came back to him, bringing rage, hatred, remorse, and consternation. He looked around for Mitch who had left no note, but Drake could tell from the condition of Potter's bed and the mess in the kitchen that Mitch had left in a hurry.

Well, this gives me time to try to sort things out, Drake thought to himself.

What should I do next? Whatever I do it has to be in concert with Mitch. He wondered if they should contact Trask immediately, confess the loss, and try to work out a settlement of some kind. He didn't worry about being sued because he had no tangible assets to speak of; but he realized that, if Trask could convince the police to file a criminal suit against him, he might do some jail time.

Even so, he hoped that most of the manuscript still in Trask's hands would serve the original purpose. If it could be dated thirty years or more before Joseph Smith published the Book of Mormon, the Mormon Church would collapse.

After re-heating Mitch's left-over coffee, Drake showered, dressed, stopped by for eggs over easy at his usual café, and took a series of buses to the University of Chicago. On his way, he once more bemoaned the fact that his computer had never been fixed since its recent crash.

At the main University of Chicago library, his old Berkeley library card permitted entry. He went to one of the many computer terminals that could yield information on any topic, by any author, held in books on the shelves of this magnificent library and many other libraries as well.

His search took him to several sources that unfolded the complexities of doing forensic examinations on old manuscripts. Then he called up the greater Chicago area yellow pages. There was only one name listed under "Forensic Analyst: Document Verification." He noted the address and telephone number, then made his way to a quiet spot to think, undisturbed.

So far, this seems almost too easy, he thought. *But the rest'll be much harder. I wonder how much time such an analysis will take to settle things one way or another? Time shouldn't be a problem unless Trask pushes legal action. Probable cost? Where would I get the money?*

He realized that all this conjecture meant nothing if Trask would not cooperate. *Will Trask refuse to have anything more to do with Mitch? Or with me? Trask could easily pursue his own agenda and tell Potter and his feckless friend where to go.*

After three hours in the library, Drake knew Potter would now be home from work. He telephoned.

"Where the hell have you been?" Mitch exploded.

"I'm at the University of Chicago library, doing some research on document verification. I'll give you all the details when I get back, which should be in about an hour and a half."

"You stupid jerk! You don't have a document to verify!"

"Hey, Mitch. I don't blame you for being mad. But wait'll you hear what I've learned. I think there's a way out of the mess I've created. See you as soon as the Chicago Transit Authority permits."

Pat Donavan called Ririe at his home to tell him Drake had checked out of his motel.

"That's an interesting development, Pat. How'd you learn about it?"

"I tried to contact him at his motel to ask him some questions I should've asked earlier and perhaps get some better insights into him."

"You're really going out of your way, Pat, and I appreciate what you're doing."

"I would do just about anything for you, Brother Tony."

Ririe then told him of Drake's call to the Salt Lake Police

Department and Sgt. Sorensen's call to Garth Garrick. They agreed that the manuscript was no longer in Drake's hands. Ririe then called Garrick and asked him to contact President Cannon at once. "Have him call me at home."

When Cannon called, Ririe asked, "Hank, how're things in Denver?"

"Just great, Tony. But I've a gut feeling you have something more important on your mind. What's up?"

"I can't give you the details by phone, Hank. No change in either President Wood or President Lund. But something's come up that requires your presence here just as soon as you can make it after your Sunday meetings."

"I have a reservation on the first plane out Monday morning. I could be in the office by noon. That soon enough?"

"Hank, there's a flight out at two which you should be able to catch after your last meeting on Sunday. Let your children or whoever might be traveling with you catch the Monday flight. Let others take care of whatever church matters must be handled after that meeting. But if that flight is full, charter an executive jet."

"Wow, Tony. Sounds like something big. Okay, count on me being in your home Sunday about five or six."

"I can always count on you, Hank. But keep the reason for your change of plans to yourself. Just say you've run out of your blood pressure medicine and need to get home."

"From your tone of voice, Tony, I'm going to need extra blood pressure medicine."

"Yes, and maybe some tranquilizers for both of us."

A Church Security driver met Cannon and his wife, Allison, at the airport, stopped at their home where Hank escorted his wife inside, and then drove the counselor to Ririe's home.

"Good to see you, Hank. Hope I haven't given you heartburn with my cryptic message yesterday." Ririe's smile belied his concern. "How'd things go in Denver?"

"Tony, can we just cut to the reason I'm here?"

Ririe gave him an account of the developments since the previous Monday, withholding no detail.

Cannon listened without speaking, stunned, but absorbing the unbelievable information. Then he summarized aloud what he had just heard to see if he had the facts straight. Unfortunately, he did. Cannon then declared with his characteristic forcefulness, "Ed Hayes ought to be excommunicated immediately."

Ririe made an important point: Hayes must have a fair opportunity to present his side of the story. Cannon reluctantly agreed. Then he asked, "If Ed really intends to destroy the manuscript, what does that say about his testimony of the Book of Mormon?"

"It says his testimony is paper thin," Ririe responded wryly.

Cannon also foresaw that destroying the manuscript would not eliminate the problem. The owners—Sherman Drake and Mitchell Potter—would submit the remaining part for forensic analysis. If that analysis proved the document fake, that fact alone wouldn't prove the Book of Mormon to be true. Cannon knew that a person's belief in the Book of Mormon came from a personal testimony that grows from thoughtful reading, humble prayer, and application of its teachings.

"But what if the forensic analysis substantiates the claim that the document antedates the publication of the Book of Mormon?" Cannon asked.

"Hank, that'd be impossible," Ririe responded, "because the Book of Mormon is genuine. It is what Joseph Smith and millions of others have claimed it to be."

"Yes, but—" And Hank Cannon fell silent.

CHAPTER TWENTY-THREE

APPRENTICESHIP OF DOUBT

Saturday, 16 May 2020

In spite of the strain of events since their first meeting on the preceding Tuesday, Ririe and Belnap met again Saturday evening to continue the account of Belnap's spiritual journey. Belnap reminded Ririe that Harriet Hudson had interrupted their conversation at the point where Belnap said he'd decided to endure the lesser pain involved by staying in the Church.

"I was sustained in part by my father telling me, 'He who has not served an apprenticeship of doubt has not earned the right of belief.' Maybe belief will come, I thought, because I certainly had my doubts. Whether or not I was serving an apprenticeship, I didn't know."

"But your apprenticeship has long since been completed, has it not?"

"Yes, but that's not to say some scriptural passages don't still cause me to scratch my head."

Ririe admitted to a little head scratching of his own.

Belnap continued, "Harold Bartholomew, the institute director, was very helpful. He helped me understand that the various disciplines had unique paths to truth—and that included religion. Mathematics—regarded by some as the queen of the sciences and by others as its handmaiden—has its own logic. A mathematician once wrote, 'Following the rules consistently constitutes the sine qua non of pure mathematics.'"

"Isn't that true of religion?"

"Yes, but not so strictly. At any rate, Tony, we then moved on to the methods of determining truth in the physical sciences. In the physical sciences, mathematics becomes a tool rather than a study in itself. Using that tool as one performs experiments, one can deduce truths such as the relationship in gases between pressure, volume, and temperature. Remember that from high school?"

"Vaguely."

"The point I want to make is this: the allowable margin for error is only slightly greater for physical truths than for mathematical truths."

"I'll take your word for that."

"However, the biological sciences, at the practical level, are not quite as exact as the physical sciences. A cursory look through the most recent edition of the AMA Drug Evaluations quickly tells you that there are few if any one-to-one relationships between a diagnosed health condition and a prescribed remedy."

"How well I know! If I take a motion sickness pill, I fall asleep. Marybeth, on the other hand, can take two at once and still be alert."

"I can relate to that," Belnap responded. "But let's move on to the behavioral sciences. With innumerable and often uncontrollable variables at work, those exacting standards of proof are impossible to obtain in such disciplines as sociology and psychology.

"Sociologists, for example, have reported the differential divorce rates among partners of similar and dissimilar religious backgrounds. They assert that marriages where both partners are of the same faith have a greater chance of success than marriages between partners from widely different religious traditions. But that doesn't permit us to say that the marriage between this Jane Roe, of a fundamentalist

Protestant faith, and that John Doe, of a strong non-Christian faith, will perforce end in divorce. We can only say that, out of one hundred such marriages, a given percentage failed in the past. They compare that rate of failure with that of one hundred marriages between couples of the same religion and find that the latter group has a statistically greater chance of success than the former."

"Yes, I've quoted those figures many times in my talks on marriage," Tony said.

"Such researchers use tables and tell us that the probability of obtaining these differences by chance alone is, say, .05. They regard that as a significant difference. Put another way, they say that if they repeated the same experiment one hundred times, they would get, by chance factors alone, the results they originally obtained only five times.

"Behavioral scientists regard such findings as significant, but the physical and biological scientists would scoff at such claims in their fields. Would you take a flight to New York, if you knew that five out of one hundred such flights wouldn't make it safely?"

"That very clearly makes your point," Ririe conceded.

"But much of the research done in psychology and sociology relies on that margin. And so there are unique approaches to truth in each broad category of the disciplines. Have I lost you anywhere along the line, Tony?" Grant Belnap asked with a straight face.

"Almost, a time or two, but in the main I've been able to follow you. I guess you're now going to tell me that validating truth in religion takes an entirely different tack. Am I right?"

"As always, you're one step ahead of me, Tony." And Grant Belnap continued.

"Just as there are different methods of approaching truth in the various disciplines, so there can be yet a different method

of inquiry in religious matters. And just as the met'
physicist can't be applied directly to the study of sociolo_,
example, so the methods of none of them are directly applic-
able to religious faith; the standards of proof in matters of faith
are unique to that field."

"Now you're going to tell me about scientific objectivity."

"Yes, scientific objectivity. Omitting the biases of the scientific investigator—what the scientist *hopes* he'll find—is an
absolute must in the sciences. But does that necessarily mean
it has to be omitted from the search for spiritual reality?"

"Probably not."

"William James would agree with you. More than a century
ago he declared, 'We have the right to believe at our own risk
any hypothesis that is live enough to tempt our will.' He wrote
that, by the way, in a book titled, *The Will to Believe.*"

"*The Will to Believe.* I like the thought that title conveys."

Belnap continued. "Harold Bartholomew convinced me
that the hypothesis of immortality is live enough to tempt one's
will. And because that and related hypotheses are so very live,
I could replace scientific objectivity with faith. And, Tony, you
have known since childhood what Paul wrote about faith."

"The substance of things hoped for and the evidence of
things not seen."

"At about that time I wrote a paraphrase of Paul's definition
that goes something like this. Faith is the ability to tolerate
ambiguity and the facility to make closure on the basis of
partial evidence."

"Tolerate ambiguity? Yes, I think I understand that one."

Belnap smiled and continued, "The ability to tolerate ambiguity is essential. The premature demanding of final
answers—absolute proof, if you will—where final answers and
absolute proof are hard to obtain has led many an unwary individual along unhappy paths.

"And so, by tolerating ambiguity," Belnap continued, "I came to realize that the Bible was the story of events as recorded by honest men in an attempt to account for the unaccountable. They interpreted reality as they saw it."

"But we say that we believe the Bible to be the word of God!"

"Only as far as it is translated correctly. Its writers were trying to make sense out of the lives they were experiencing in their time and place. The Bible is full of great moral truths, yet is replete with contradictions. The great moral truths come from on high, while the contradictions are the works of men. And, as I might have mentioned a few days ago, I realized that the Bible is not a handbook of geology."

"But, at the very least the Bible is a valuable handbook of life. Wouldn't you agree?"

"I agree with one stipulation. The reader of the Bible must think. It was about that time I read some of Emily Dickinson's poems, one of which struck me so forcefully I memorized it."

Tell all the Truth but tell it slant -
Success in Circuit lies

Too bright for our infirm Delight
The Truth's superb surprise

As Lightning to the Children eased
With explanation kind

The Truth must dazzle gradually
Or every man be blind –

Ririe repeated thoughtfully, "'The truth must dazzle gradually, or every man be blind.' Very sensitive."

"Sensitive, indeed."

"Yes, but we must ponder those verses to get their full significance," Ririe cautioned.

"As is true of most thought-provoking verses. Well, Harold and I worked out something of a formula for measuring the value of a given religious concept or belief that combined external evidence, practical application, a pure heart, and a desire to believe. We came to the conclusion that desiring to believe was perfectly legitimate. While the hopes for a certain outcome of a pure scientist must not be allowed to color his findings, the hopes of the religious investigator are very much a part of the equation."

Ririe asked, "But wouldn't such an approach permit a person of any denomination to verify the teachings of his or her church in the same way?"

"Yes, of course. What makes it different for us is the source we claim for the restored gospel: heavenly messengers sent from on high."

"So, how do *you* know the Book of Mormon is what it claims to be?" Ririe asked his friend and colleague. Ririe wanted to ask how his answer would fit in with his first 'what if' of a few days earlier.

"To answer that question I must repeat the formula I just mentioned: External evidence, practical application, a pure heart, and a desire to believe can lead one to a conviction of spiritual truth."

He continued, "I know the Book of Mormon is true by the scholarly research, such as Wordprints. Research increases every year on evidences of the truth of the Book of Mormon. More important is the validity of its contents when I practice the truths it teaches. The pure-heart aspect refers to having one's life in order, that is, free from sin. While I'm not completely sinless, I am morally and sexually pure. I know the

Book of Mormon is true because I have read it, studied it, prayed about it, and I want to believe it. I know it's true because I have applied the teachings of Alma when he told his listeners, 'even if ye can no more than desire to believe.' And you know the rest of that quotation from the 32nd Chapter of Alma. I know it's true because I responded to the exhortation of Moroni to 'ask God, the Eternal Father, in the name of Christ, if these things are not true.' In that manner I've received the confirmation of the Holy Spirit that the Book of Mormon is true."

"That is a truly remarkable account, Grant. I admire your insights, your openness with me, and the strength of your faith. I imagine my profession as a CPA didn't lead me to have doubts. But haven't you left something out?"

"Yes, of course, there's a lot more to arriving at a sustainable set of beliefs than what I have just told you. We've been talking about so-called scientific truths and the means of finding them as compared with religious truths. But what about the philosophers? They've been trying to make sense out of our confusing world for centuries, if not millennia. Various schools of philosophy, some older than the Old Testament and some newer than our parents, have tried to come to an understanding of the question, 'What does it all mean?' Some speak of determinism, others of indeterminism. Some speak of absolute truth, others of relative or situational truth. Some see orderliness in the universe while others perceive widespread disorder. And, I must admit, there is some validity in all their approaches. Then there is humanism, which I think of as a religion without a god. It has many good points in its value system: But without a supreme being, what is man but an accident? When the humanists say that life, as we know it, is doomed to extinction, that nothing fine, noble, beautiful, heroic, or insightful will survive an ultimate fiery and final end, I rebel."

Tony Ririe reflected during a moment of silence between the two men. "Grant, talking with you, listening to you, has been an eye-opening experience for me. I must admit that I was shaken for a time after I visited with Pat Donovan last Monday. Yes, life has meaning. The Book of Mormon helps us to understand that meaning. And so I have no fears about what the Drakes of this world will do or say or claim. That document he brought to Salt Lake doesn't scare me. I have no doubt it will be proven false. In the meantime, what do we do next? What steps should we take with respect to Ed Hayes and his apparently unwise involvement with the manuscript? And another thing bothers me. If Ed Hayes really gets his hands on that manuscript, will he destroy it? And does that mean he believed it to be genuine? If so, what does that say about his testimony?"

It was Belnap's turn to reflect. Finally he answered, "I see your point about Elder Hayes's testimony. His alleged actions don't speak well for his belief in the authenticity of the Book of Mormon. What steps to take next? I think we both know what they should be. I'll help you in any way you want me to, but you call the shots, Tony. I see my role in all this as very much subordinate to yours."

"Yes, the buck stops here, Grant," Ririe acknowledged. "But I'm glad to have you on my team. Of course I'll call on you and draw upon your sound advice every step of the way. But I have one request: Please volunteer your advice at any time. Don't wait for me to ask."

"Thank you, Tony. Your trust in me is something I treasure. And speaking of trust, I almost left out the most important aspect of my journey from certainty to doubt and back to a different kind of certainty. I married Mattie just after we both graduated from Harvard. She did more than anyone else to help me make sense out of my world. During our courtship and marriage, I could talk with her, find a listening and understanding ear, and strength beyond compare. When I was on the point of doubting everything, she helped me resolve the many conflicts I was experiencing. She kept me in the Church. To the day she died, she was true to the Church, true to me, and true to the truth."

Both men had tears in their eyes as they parted.

Grant Belnap stayed in his empty home while Anthony Ririe returned to a warm welcome from his wife. Before he finally fell asleep that night, Ririe reflected on his discussion with Grant Belnap. He realized that he himself was almost the model of the iron-rodder Belnap had described. He believed strongly in the word of God as found in the scriptures. He found security in accepting at face value what the holy books told him. He knew that once you start to question some parts of the scriptures you could move by degrees, hardly aware of the movement, to the point where you question more and more. Where do you stop? Some don't stop until they question the divine calling of Joseph Smith; others wind up questioning the divinity of the Savior. Still others come to doubt the very existence of God.

Yes, he decided silently, *I'm very comfortable being an iron-rodder. The difference between Grant and me in the matter of our faith is somewhat analogous to our current marital situations. Although he most likely will marry again before too long, he is alone with only himself for comfort and understanding, while I have the blessings of my Marybeth.*

With that he fell asleep, with his source of comfort and blessings warmly beside him.

CHAPTER TWENTY-FOUR

FACES OF SUNDAY

Sunday, 17 May 2020

Sunday is many things to many people: outdoor recreation, indoor TV sports, sleeping in, or sleeping it off—and, for the faithful of many persuasions, going to church.

For Patrick J. Donavan, Bishop of the Catholic Diocese of Salt Lake City, the highlight of Sunday, 17 May 2020, was celebrating Mass in the Cathedral of the Madeleine.

Built on land purchased in February 1890, the cathedral was dedicated on August 15, 1909. From 1991 to 1993 a complete renovation and restoration of the interior had been completed at a cost of $9.7 million. This involved disassembling and cleaning all of the stained glass windows piece by piece and remounting them in new lead strips and framing. The murals, dimmed with the accumulation of the years, were cleaned and, where necessary, restored. The pews were rearranged to accommodate the relocation of the altar, resulting in a reduction of seating capacity from 1,000 to 950 seats. Other restorative measures had been taken during the years preceding Bishop Donavan's episcopate.

As he vested for Mass, Bishop Donavan reflected on the faithfulness of his predecessors and their flocks. The smallest contributions from the poorest members were as great in the sight of God as the major donations that actually made the cathedral and its furnishings possible.

He loved this cathedral—old in western America, but new by European standards. The vaulted ceilings, the murals on walls and ceilings, the magnificent stained-glass windows, the feeling of the presence of God as he prepared himself, outwardly and inwardly—these and much more enriched the soul of this dedicated servant of God.

The deacon, who would lead the procession and assist him through the Mass, watched Bishop Donavan don his plain white full-length alb with its long sleeves, and his ornate sleeveless chasuble, which had a magnificent cross on the back. Then came his skullcap and his gently peaked miter, the symbols of his office. Lastly, he took up his staff, which indicated his role as shepherd of the flock. While all this was taking place, the worshippers were listening to the prelude to the Eucharist, or communion service, being played on the magnificent seventy-seven-rank cathedral organ by a talented and well-trained organist.

The twenty-voice choir sang the processional hymn as they walked up the main aisle from the vestibule to their location behind the screen separating the altar from the tabernacle, the place where the consecrated hosts—the wafers and wine—from previous services are kept.

The deacon, carrying the Lectionary—which contained the words of the service—high above his head with both hands, followed the choir. He was followed by the cross bearer and then by an altar boy and an altar girl walking side by side. Last came Bishop Patrick J. Donavan. Except for the choir, all members of the procession stood behind the altar facing the congregation. The bishop then bowed and kissed the altar.

The Mass began with the Liturgy of the Word, in the manner of the Universal Church. There were prayers, responses from the large congregation, hymns, and three scripture readings, one from the Old Testament, another selected from one of the Epistles, and the third from one of the Gospels. The homily, or sermon, by Bishop Donavan drew its lesson from those scriptures featuring the love of Christ. The bishop asked if all present could understand the extent of the love Jesus Christ had for all of us—great enough to die for us—to save us from our sins. Then he asked, "Do you love Christ enough, not to die for Him, but to live for Him? Enough to practice His precepts and example? Enough to demonstrate love for wives, husbands, parents, children, siblings, and others by the kindness shown toward them?" He carried out his theme with practical examples of how this could be done.

The congregation, now standing, made their profession of faith by reciting the Nicene Creed. The bread and wine and the monetary gifts of God's people were brought to the altar and presented to God. Then followed the Liturgy of the Eucharist, which included the words the Lord had spoken when he broke bread with his disciples.

Take this, all of you, and eat it:
this is my Body which will be given for you.
And then the Lord took the cup of wine and said:
Take this, all of you, and drink from it:
this is the cup of my Blood,
the Blood of the new and everlasting covenant.
It will be shed for you and for all
so that sins may be forgiven.
Do this in memory of me.

After the hosts had been consecrated to become the Body of Christ and after the wine had been consecrated to become the Blood of Christ, the faithful came forward to receive the blessed sacrament of Holy Communion from the Bishop and the Eucharistic ministers.

Bishop Donavan then announced, "The Mass is ended. Go in peace to love and serve the Lord by serving and loving one another."

To which the congregation responded, "Thanks be to God."

As Bishop Donavan followed the recessional, he felt again the divine presence. He sensed it reflected in the lives of his communicants, whom he blessed with the sign of the cross as he walked by. He felt it in the magnificent music of the final hymn and the organ postlude, and he felt it within himself, having once again partaken of the Body and Blood of Christ.

At about the same time that their good friend, Bishop Donavan, was officiating at Mass, Anthony and Marybeth Ririe were slowly making their way into the chapel of their local ward. Although they attended services there whenever they weren't on official assignment elsewhere in this worldwide Church, their fellow ward members always wanted to shake their hands, exchange a few words, and feel the spirit which seemed to surround them. This made the process of getting seated somewhat lengthy.

Standard practice in the Mormon Church calls for such a high-ranking official to sit on the stand near the local ward bishop. But Tony Ririe always insisted that he and his wife sit in the congregation.

Unobtrusive organ music, neither too loud nor too soft, was being played by one of the few remaining competent organists in the Church. The decline of musical talent caused by the electronic era had long alarmed Tony Ririe. He hoped the new push by the Church, calling for young people to serve a "Talent Development Mission," would reverse that trend.

At the appointed hour the bishop stood, reverently welcomed the congregation, asked the members to note the announcements on the printed program, and then he sat down. He felt there was no need for him to tell them the name and page number of the hymns—they were posted on the wall, and listed in the program. Nor did he announce the name of the person assigned earlier to offer the invocation since her name was also on the printed program.

After the opening hymn, in which the congregation entered with subdued enthusiasm, the sister who had been asked to pray invoked the Spirit of the Lord to be present with those who would speak, provide music, and listen. Her short and specific prayer was followed by some ward business and a sacrament hymn.

The young Aaronic Priesthood holders conducted the administration of the Sacrament of the Lord's Supper in an orderly, reverent manner. Each person in the congregation had the opportunity to partake of the bread and water, which symbolized the flesh and blood of the Savior—His sacrifice for all.

Then the bishop gave a brief biographical note on each of the three speakers so the congregation would know more than just their names.

The addresses were well prepared. Two fifteen-year-olds, a boy and a girl, gave short, original, and thought-provoking messages. They looked their audience in the eye with minimal reliance on notes. When they cited scriptures, they quoted from memory.

Following a polished musical number, the main speaker delivered a relevant message of instruction, hope, and inspiration.

Without further announcement from the bishop, the closing hymn followed, and the brother who gave the benediction expressed thanks for each of the speakers and for the music. He also asked the blessings of the Lord to accompany all present throughout this Sabbath day and the days ahead.

President Anthony J. Ririe felt that he and Marybeth had just attended a perfect sacrament meeting.

CHAPTER TWENTY-FIVE

PROFANE AND SACRED

Harriet Hudson—clad in bathrobe and slippers—that same Sunday tuned her apartment TV to the Mormon Tabernacle Choir program. Although she hated much about the Mormon Church, she had always loved the Tabernacle Choir. She didn't know that this choir of 350 voices had been on the air for consecutive Sundays for more than 90 years. Nor did she know that the Tabernacle organ contained more than 12,000 pipes. What she did know was that she was always moved by that weekly event. At the end of the broadcast, she quickly turned off her TV before the intruding commercial broke the mood. She found herself crying, wondering if something precious was missing from her life, and groped desperately in her refrigerator for a can of beer. Soon, she knew, she would be oblivious to all cares—worldly and otherworldly alike.

In Denver that Sunday morning, Henry Cannon, second counselor in the First Presidency, was presiding at an area conference in the New Mile High Stadium where more than fifty thousand Latter-day Saints were seated in the northern tier of seats. A podium had been erected where hash marks on the fifty-yard line would have been. The magnificent public address system permitted all to hear without difficulty.

A choir drawn from several stakes in the immediate area presented some wonderfully stirring numbers. There had been a time when such choirs were limited to singing Mormon hymns, but that restriction had been lifted years earlier. Henry Cannon and all present were moved by the choir's rendition of

"The Hallelujah Chorus" from *The Mount of Olives* by Beethoven.

During the addresses by those accompanying him, President Cannon's thoughts returned to Tony Ririe's phone call the day before. *What was behind that call?* Ririe had told him there had been no change in the health of either President Wood or President Lund. *Had there been another terrorist threat to the Church in South America? Were our missionaries about to be declared persona non grata by some dictatorship somewhere? Had one of the Twelve stumbled? And what did it say about Ririe's state of mind that he would refuse to discuss it over the phone? Was Ririe becoming as paranoid as Hayes? Or was there a serious problem with internal security?*

Then it was time for him to deliver the major address—a sermon. He congratulated "all concerned with the preparations for this great conference." He commented on the power of the music they had just heard, calling attention to the fact that God had inspired composers of many faiths in the creation of truly magnificent music. He told the choir members that they were now well-prepared to sing with the angels of heaven, but they would have to wait until they were invited to join that ethereal choir.

Then he spoke frankly of the role of the counselors in the First Presidency at a time when the President himself was unable to participate in the governance of the Church. He pointed out what some of his predecessors had asserted many years before under similar circumstances. "The two counselors have full authority to press forward in the work of the Lord in consultation with the Quorum of the Twelve."

After other relevant remarks, and after bearing a strong testimony of the truth—not the *truthfulness*—of The Book of Mormon and the divine calling and mission of the Prophet Joseph Smith and all of his successors, he sat down and drank in the music of the choir as they sang Handel's "Worthy Is the Lamb."

Cannon had previously asked one of the stake presidents to drive him and Allison directly to the airport. They had just enough time to make the two o'clock flight back to Salt Lake City and to the surprise of his life.

In the meantime, Sherman Drake and Mitchell Potter fidgeted in their Des Plaines apartment, trying to figure out how to break the news of the loss of the document to its owner, Albert Trask.

"I'm so angry I can't think," Drake snarled. "I'm angry with myself and mad as hell at the Mormons who stole that thing. What can we possibly tell Trask?"

"If we let rage do our thinking for us, we won't be able to work our way out of this mess," Potter responded.

"One of my foster parents—I forget which one—used to say, 'When in doubt, tell the truth.' Maybe that's the way we should go," Drake suggested.

"I can't think of a better way."

With that, Potter called Trask and made an appointment to meet him at his home that evening.

CHAPTER TWENTY-SIX

HIGH ON HIS LIST

Monday, 18 May 2020

Ririe, Cannon, Belnap, and Garrick met again in Belnap's office early Monday morning. Garrick, an unpleasant combination of obsequiousness and officiousness, reported that Hayes and his wife, Stephanie, were expected back from New York on Tuesday afternoon, the 19th; and because there were no signs of forced entry at the motel room and no other evidence of theft, the Salt Lake police had put Drake's case on hold. He also reported Collins's death, the negative search of Collins's car, and his suspicions about Orvin Collins's possible involvement in the disappearance of the manuscript. He also pointed out that Elder Hayes was out of town when the theft most likely occurred.

"Brother Garrick, you've made some damning accusations not only about a dead man, but also about Elder Hayes in saying he ordered you to steal that document," Belnap commented. "Won't he be likely to deny giving you any such order when he's confronted, leaving us with your word against his?"

"Yes, sir. That's a real possibility." Garrick took out his handkerchief and nervously wiped his brow. Then he continued with an air of triumph: "But I have it on tape."

Ririe and Belnap looked at each other. Each felt that Garrick's bugging Hayes was equally unsavory, to say the least.

"Brother Garrick," Ririe instructed, "I want those tapes as soon as you can get them to my office. Hank, I want you to listen to them with me. It's imperative that we both have all the facts before Elder Hayes returns. That gives us only today and tomorrow to work out our strategy before Hank and I have to face Elder Hayes on Wednesday. How does that sound to the three of you? You first, Hank."

"Sounds right to me. But what about Joseph Lund? Shouldn't the President of the Quorum of the Twelve be informed?"

"Of course. I'll visit him this evening. Grant, what are your thoughts?"

"Seeing President Lund is imperative. Other than that, we do have some strategy to work out and we'll need that time."

"And your reactions, Brother Garrick?"

Garth Garrick, visibly pleased at being included, responded, "Brethren, I'm honored that you'd ask for my opinion. Yes, I agree entirely with what has been proposed so far. But it'll take a couple of hours to assemble the relevant parts of my tapes. You don't want to listen to a lot of unrelated stuff."

Tony Ririe nodded and rose. Ririe, Cannon, and Garrick went directly to their offices while Belnap stopped at Norma's desk.

Belnap smiled down at Norma. "I know I don't have to say this but I'm going to say it anyway, by way of reinforcing your very good instincts. You must tell no one of the meeting just held in my office."

"Message received, Elder Belnap. You have several calls to return."

"Yes, I'll go to work on them now. Norma, you will never know how truly grateful I am to have such a secretary. God bless you."

As he returned to his office, the thought struck him for the first time that, should he ever consider remarrying, Norma Ashcraft would be high on his list.

CHAPTER TWENTY-SEVEN

NORMA ASHCRAFT

Monday, 18 May 2020

At home Monday evening, Norma Ashcraft, a relatively young widow, reflected on the meeting held in her boss's office that day, especially on Elder Belnap's parting comment to her. In a meditative mood, she took her simple supper out to the balcony of her condo on the East Bench and ate as she watched the sun sink toward the Great Salt Lake. She thought about her mission to the New England area and wondered how life would've unfolded had she not been called to that particular mission as a young woman.

She remembered her parents and her brothers and sisters. What a joy to have been raised in a large and largely faithful Latter-day Saint family! She had grown up on a small farm just outside the city limits of Spanish Fork, Utah. She recalled the excellent education she received in the public schools, the weddings of her older brothers and sisters, her own marriage. Tears stung her eyes,

Both she and her high school sweetheart, Benjamin Ashcraft, had known since they were in the eleventh grade that they would marry some day. They had married within three months of his return from his mission. During his absence, Norma had gone to a nearby trade school where she honed the skills learned in high school and became an excellent office worker and secretary, complete with all the mandatory computer skills.

She recalled with fondness the showers her family and

friends had arranged, the wedding itself in the Spanish Fork Temple, and the weeks of wedded bliss before that shattering phone message—Ben had been killed in a trench cave-in while working for his father's small construction company.

It took months for the shock, disbelief, and grief to subside. Then she decided that she, too, would serve a mission. She enjoyed her experience. For the first six months, she and her companion were assigned to a small town in Rhode Island where contacts leading to conversions were very sparse. Then she was transferred to the mission office where her skills as an organizer, word processor, and programmer won high praise from her mission president.

Shortly before she was released at the end of her eighteen-month call, an apostle on a mission tour told her that her mission president had praised her excellent work and skills. He suggested that she apply for a position at church headquarters upon her release and to use his name as a reference.

She did and was hired as a new member of the secretarial pool. Within a few months she was promoted to be full-time secretary to the chairman of the Missionary Committee where she served for several years. A year after Grant Belnap was called to be a member of the Quorum of the Twelve, her supervisor glumly told her that she was being transferred to Belnap's office. She enjoyed this new job—so much, in fact, that she had become skilled at not acknowledging the depths of, or the reason for, that enjoyment.

She carried her dishes quickly into the kitchen and switched on her computer, forcing herself to refocus her talent for investing and trading in the stock market, using her latest state-of-the-art computer. She had almost backed into her investment activities, taking a flutter when a friend had dared her to try her hand. Success came quickly, thanks to her ability to analyze large amounts of data and to make almost intuitive decisions. Her portfolio had doubled, then doubled again. She could have lived on the profits from her sagacious investments, but she felt no desire to do so. She lived for her work and her boss. She often wondered to herself if she'd been trying to serve both God and mammon. Her last car was an expensive luxury model. Was she trying to prove something to the male power structure within which she moved every working moment? A power structure in which women continued to play subordinate roles?

In spite of his involvement with the document crisis, Grant Belnap left on 25 May for a three-week assignment to Africa, during which he found himself thinking of his secretary. It finally dawned on him that Norma was the best-dressed female employee in the building. *How can she afford those clothes on what the Church pays her?* he wondered. *But it isn't her clothes that attract me—it is her personality, her cheerfulness, her very self!*

He reflected on how both Ririe and Cannon had encouraged him to remarry as soon as he was ready.

Upon returning from that African assignment about the middle of June, he went to his office early on a Monday, usually a quiet day at 47 East South Temple. Norma Ashcraft, who had been in his thoughts during his entire trip, had arrived earlier than usual, and was working at her desk when he walked into the office.

"Good morning, Norma," Elder Belnap said with a smile. "My goodness, you certainly are here bright and early. Another nice new outfit, right?"

"I knew you'd come in early. You always do after a long trip." She ignored his mention of her clothing.

Her smile, the tone of her voice, and her general ambiance caused Belnap to think, just for a moment, how wonderful it would be to take her in his arms. Then Norma dropped the bomb.

"Elder Belnap, I'd like to be transferred to some other office, preferably not in this building."

Belnap was speechless, a unique experience for him. When he finally could speak he stammered, "Why, Norma? You know how much I depend upon you."

"May I be perfectly honest and frank, Elder Belnap? It's because, although I fought it every step of the way, I've fallen in love with you."

He paused briefly and then spoke softly but with unmistakable sincerity, "I'm pleased that's your reason for wanting a transfer, because I've fallen in love with you, too. Norma, dear Norma, will you marry me?"

"Yes, yes!" Her voice broke as they exchanged a long kiss and a longer embrace. Grant broke the embrace and silence to look at her wonderful face. His next words reflected her own thoughts. "Who do we tell first?"

"President Ririe?"

"My thought exactly. May I use your phone to call Beverly and find out how soon President Ririe might be able to see us?"

They walked to the elevator without touching one another. When Beverly escorted them into Ririe's inner office, they took one another by the hand and walked up to the smiling Tony Ririe. Ririe rose from his chair, walked around his desk, took each one by the hand, and then twinkled, "Bless you, my children."

Ririe told them he had seen this coming and was delighted. In fact, he wondered why it had taken Grant so long. He suggested that Norma take an immediate leave of absence until the time of the wedding. After the wedding she could resign with accrued pension rights fully intact. Neither he nor Belnap had any idea she didn't need a pension. A few days later the newly engaged couple asked President Ririe to perform the marriage in the Salt Lake Temple on the 23rd of July.

Grant Belnap had a hard time adjusting to someone other than Norma at her post. Norma, for her part, had a hard time staying away from the office, even with all of the arrangements she needed to make for the wedding. But they both survived— he immersed in Church affairs, and she even busier with her investments. They saw each other frequently but never alone except for driving to Spanish Fork to break the news to Norma's parents who were overwhelmed and overjoyed. Over the weeks the engaged couple had dinner with Tony and Marybeth Ririe, with Hank and Allison Cannon, and with a few other close friends.

Norma's church headquarters friends immediately deduced the news from her leave of absence and were ecstatic when she confirmed it. Typical bridal showers were out of the question, but Norma did agree to a big women-only party.

For his part, Grant Belnap was busy with the ruts and bumps of his church duties. But his mind was never far from concern about the mysterious document.

CHAPTER TWENTY-EIGHT

SIZING UP GARRICK

Monday, 18 May 2020

When Tony Ririe returned to his office from meeting with Cannon, Belnap, and Garrick, he called President Lund's home, where his daughter answered.

"Hello, Margaret. This is Tony Ririe."

"Yes, President Ririe. Dad was just talking about you. I'll put him on."

"Not so fast, Margaret. How are you? And how is he?" Ririe asked.

"Thanks for asking, President. I never felt better. But I can't say the same for Dad. I think he's slowly going downhill. Nothing specific I can detect except that he's responding more slowly when I talk to him."

"I'm genuinely sorry to hear that. Do you think he'd be up to a visit from President Cannon and me in about an hour? There are some things we need to discuss with him—things we don't want to deal with over the phone."

"He always perks up after you've been here, President, so I'm sure he'd love to see you both. But I'll ask."

In a moment she relayed word that President Lund would be very pleased to see them.

Ririe took care of several matters on his desk, returned a couple of phone calls, called Marybeth to tell her he would be late for supper, and then called Garth Garrick.

"Brother Garrick, Tony Ririe here. Would you be available to ride shotgun for me in fifteen minutes?"

"President, I'm at your service, day or night. Should I meet you at your office or your car?"

"Let's make it the car. President Cannon will ride with us."

"Right. I'll be waiting at your car."

And waiting he was—unhappy, concerned, worried, tired from a sleepless night, but outwardly calm.

Ririe asked Garrick to drive and got in the passenger seat. Cannon took the rear seat.

"We need to talk with President Lund, Brother Garrick, so that's where we're headed," he began. "I thought I'd take this opportunity to talk things over with you."

Garrick licked his lips nervously. "President, I'm glad you asked me to drive you today. I know my career as head of Church Security is in danger because of my actions."

"May I be informal and call you Garth?"

"Of course, President."

"Garth, if what you've told President Cannon, Elder Belnap, and me about Elder Hayes holds up, I doubt that your career is in danger. Perhaps when I'm finished at President Lund's, we can listen to the relevant parts of the tapes you say you have. In the meantime I've been rethinking your statements about my own security. That's the other reason I asked you to accompany me this afternoon—I want to get the feel of having a security man with me. So far, it's not as bad as I feared. Perhaps I can think more clearly when I don't have to worry about driving. Maybe I've been foolish in resisting your suggestions about my own security."

"Thank you, President. When this business about the manuscript and Elder Hayes's involvement is all over, I'd like to step down as head of security and be assigned as personal security to one of the Brethren."

"I think that could be arranged, Garth."

They drove on in silence for the few remaining minutes it

took to reach the Lund home high on the Avenues overlooking the city.

Margaret Perry ushered them into the living room where Joseph Lund was sitting in a recliner with a hand-knit afghan covering his legs. Ririe introduced Garrick, then suggested that Margaret and Garrick might like to wait in another room while he, Cannon, and Lund talked.

"Tony, it's always good to see you." Lund smiled. "Good to see you, too, Hank. But two times in eight days, Tony? I sense there's something quite serious on your mind. Tell me about it."

Ririe thought it was like Joseph Lund to cut off the preliminary chitchat.

"Yes, Joseph. We have a double challenge." Succinctly and clearly he explained the details of the call from Pat Donovan, the manuscript and its preliminary examination, Ririe's discussion of the matter with Grant Belnap and Hank Cannon, the theft of the manuscript, the wiretapping of his office and Belnap's home, and Elder Hayes's apparent involvement.

"Tony, that's an amazing and disturbing story. Very disturbing. Are you certain of Ed Hayes's involvement?"

"I'll be more certain later this evening. What we need to discuss with you now is where do we go from here? If Ed's up to his ears in this mess, what should be done?"

Lund touched the fingers of his two hands together and held his forefingers to his lips as he carefully considered his answer. His response was a question.

"What do you recommend, Tony?"

"I'm glad Hank's back in town. I recommend that Hank and I meet with you again as early as you're able to receive us tomorrow morning. I also recommend that Grant Belnap be present. We'll have our suggestions at that time. If I had to make a recommendation right now, based on what I believe to be the facts, I'd recommend that we confront Ed Hayes with what we think he's done, here in your home the following day, Wednesday. Would you be up to that, Joseph?"

"If I'm as well as I am right now, I could handle such a meeting. I assume, of course, Tony, that all of us would be prepared to listen respectfully to Ed's version of events."

"Yes, of course. Grant, in particular, would insist on presuming innocence until the facts prove otherwise."

Joseph Lund seemed to become more alert and animated as this conversation continued. "Brethren, let's play out two results of what most likely will be regarded by Ed Hayes as a confrontation. One, he denies what you've told me. Two, he admits to your statements but tries to defend his behavior."

Ririe reflected. "Joseph, if he denies the facts as we have presented them to you, we must be prepared to have him listen to the tapes that Garth Garrick has made. I believe his only alternative will be to admit his involvement. We must then listen to whatever rationalization he can give for his actions. Unless he can come up with some justification, which I cannot now imagine, I believe that we must bring the matter to the entire Twelve in the temple. When I say the entire Twelve, I, of course, mean you would be present. Only President Wood would be absent."

Lund turned to Cannon and asked, "Henry, would you make any changes in what Tony just suggested?"

"None whatsoever."

"Brethren, your thinking coincides with my own. I wish it were possible for me to hear the relevant parts of those tapes before our meeting with Ed Hayes so I could have time to think about the content. Is that feasible? "

"Yes, that could be done tomorrow. I had Brother Garrick drive me here today to give you a chance to hear his story, to question him, to get a feel for his integrity before you listen to his tapes. I believe he's an honest and honorable man who's been caught in a situation not of his own making."

"Bring him in and let me talk with him alone. Margaret can give you some milk and cookies in the kitchen while we talk."

After an interview of less than fifteen minutes, Lund sent Garrick for Ririe and Cannon.

CHAPTER TWENTY-NINE

FACING THE MUSIC

"Tony, I agree with your assessment of Brother Garrick," Lund observed. "I feel he's an honorable man. He'll bring the relevant tapes tomorrow morning and help us listen to them. Given that, I want to repeat something we mentioned a few minutes ago, Brethren. Ed Hayes is innocent until proven guilty. We can't in good conscience convict him in our minds without hearing his side of the story. Although I'm deeply saddened by this whole matter, I'm not worried for one minute about the authenticity of that manuscript. As J. Golden Kimball observed about a century ago when his upper plate fell to the floor during a pulpit-pounding sermon, 'False as hell!'"

"President Lund, I enjoy your sense of humor, and I love and sustain you," Tony Ririe proclaimed with obvious and unfeigned affection.

"Amen," echoed Hank Cannon and Garth Garrick.

On their way back to church headquarters, Ririe, Cannon, and Garrick talked through the details of what was to follow. Ririe suggested they listen to the tapes with Joseph Lund the next day. That would free up what remained of the evening for all of them.

Garth Garrick signed out of his office in the presence of the security man on duty and returned to his home. Cannon was pleased at the opportunity to spend the evening at home.

Tony Ririe stopped in his office long enough to call his wife who reminded him that they were due at a performance of the Utah Symphony at eight.

"Honey, if your duties permit, we can still make it. I'll have a sandwich ready. You can eat in the car."

"My duties do permit—no, they demand—we go to the symphony. 'Music has charms to soothe a savage beast . . .'"

Before he could quote the second line, Marybeth gave the source of the quote—William Congreve—and noted, "I think you can stand a little soothing."

Haydn's Surprise Symphony was last on the program that evening. Ririe mused that the Surprise Symphony was analogous to what had happened a few days earlier. Haydn had wanted to awaken his audience after almost lulling them to sleep. *Maybe the Lord is giving us a wake-up call,* he thought. *Well, He certainly has my attention.*

CHAPTER THIRTY

INNOCENT UNTIL

The next day, Tuesday, 19 May 2020, Garth Garrick again drove Ririe and Cannon to the home of Joseph Lund. Garrick had spent many hours the previous night completing his work on the relevant tapes that now sat in the back seat of Ririe's car alongside a tape player.

The four men spent the better part of an hour listening. Lund heard what the others already knew: the telephone call from Pat Donovan; the existence of the now-missing document; parts of the conversations between Ririe and Belnap in the latter's home; the confrontation of Garrick in Ririe's office with Belnap present; and Garrick's assertion that he had been ordered to steal the manuscript. Most damning of all, they heard Hayes's own words, "I want you to steal that document." They also heard his unflattering evaluation of the mental status of both Presidents James D. Wood and Joseph R. Lund.

"This is one of the saddest days in my life," Lund lamented after they finished listening to the tapes. "What could Ed Hayes have been thinking?"

The other men made no response. Ririe didn't want to appear to tell Lund what the next steps should be. But he knew what they should be—first, a confrontation with Ed Hayes followed by a presentation of the facts, as they understood them, to the entire Twelve in a formal meeting in the temple.

"Brother Garrick," Lund directed in his soft voice, "I believe that President Ririe, President Cannon, and I need to discuss this matter alone."

"Of course, President," replied Garrick. "President Ririe, I'd like to walk down the hill to my office. When you and President Cannon are ready to leave, please call me and I'll have one of my men drive me up here to pick up the tapes and the equipment. That will leave you free to use your car as you wish."

"No, Garth. I want you to take my car back and wait for me to call you. I've become accustomed to being driven."

Although all of the men smiled at that light-hearted remark, the head of Church Security made his exit with a very serious look on his face.

Lund broke the silence. "Brethren, as I said before, we must give Ed Hayes every opportunity to present his side before taking any formal action. When did you say he'd be back?"

"He'll return this evening, Joseph," Hank replied.

"How do you brethren see the playing out of this tragic drama?"

Ririe answered, "First, I think it should be handled with all deliberate haste. We don't know what these enemies of the Church might do next. Second, Ed Hayes should have two opportunities to present his version of events: one before the three of us, and another before the First Presidency and the Twelve in the temple. President Wood's absence may complicate matters just a bit."

Lund looked toward Cannon and asked, "Anything to add, Hank?"

"I think Tony sized it up exactly."

Lund responded. "Where should our meeting with him take place, Tony?"

"I think we have three options: here in your home, in your office at church headquarters, or my office there. The advantage of meeting here, President, is that fewer people would know about it."

"I agree." Lund nodded. "Should Grant Belnap be included?"

"Good question, Joseph. I'm inclined to say not at our first meeting with Ed. But, of course, he would be present with the other members of the Twelve in the temple later. Do you agree?"

"Yes, Tony. Do you agree, Hank? Good. Now, about this 'all deliberate haste.' I take it you mean the first meeting with Ed Hayes should be tomorrow, with the meeting of the Presidency and the Twelve being held at the regular time the following day?"

"That's what I'd suggest, Joseph. And I think it's very important you be present at both meetings. You are Ed Hayes's line superior. Do you think you'll be equal to the events of both days?"

"If the Lord wants me to be there both days, I'll be there. If He doesn't, it won't matter what I think."

"When we meet tomorrow," added Ririe, "I suggest we have the tape player already set up. There would be no need for Garth Garrick or any technician to be present."

Joseph Lund nodded. "I just pray we're doing the right thing," he whispered.

CHAPTER THIRTY-ONE

DR. BERNARD HORNE

On Monday evening, 18 May, Drake and Potter kept their appointment with Albert Trask at his apartment in neighboring Elk Grove Village. They had spent all day wondering how to break the news about the loss of the manuscript.

"Al, this is my roommate, Sherman Drake," Potter announced as the door opened. They shook hands all around, and Trask cordially asked if they would like a drink. Drake and Potter gratefully accepted cold beers, and the three sat down in the small living room.

"It looks as if you didn't bring my partial manuscript with you," observed Trask. "Where is it?"

"It's been stolen," Drake replied. "I took it with me to Salt Lake City without Mitch's knowledge or permission and offered it to the Catholic Bishop of Salt Lake. I wanted him to use it to blast the Mormons out of the water."

Trask's chin dropped. He started to stand up but thought better of it. "Is that true, Mitch?"

"It's true," Mitch Potter admitted with a long face. "And we're here to say we're sorry. We've contacted the Salt Lake police. We want to do all we can to minimize the loss, and we acknowledge our responsibility."

"You're sorry! And it looks as if I've lost a significant part of a potentially very valuable asset!" Trask made no attempt to hide his anger. "Are you guys really leveling with me? How do I know you haven't cooked up this story so you can keep my manuscript for your own purposes?"

"I swear, Al, we have leveled with you," Potter declared convincingly.

Drake nodded his agreement.

"Okay, I guess I just have to trust you, although your story sounds phony as hell. But I like to face facts, Mitch. Let's review the facts and see where that leaves us. I loaned part of a manuscript to you, Mitch. You say Sherman took it to Salt Lake without your knowledge or permission. Sometime during your stay in Salt Lake, Sherman, you claim the manuscript was stolen and that you have reported it to the Salt Lake Police. Have you heard from them?"

"Yes, I called Sgt. Sorensen again this afternoon. He says that the matter's on hold. He says there's no evidence of forced entry at the motel, no witnesses, and the motel clerk could provide no information. Sorensen agreed to call me if anything new turned up."

"What do you make of that report, Sherman?" Trask asked.

"My guess is that they—or at least Sgt. Sorensen—are in cahoots with the Mormons. I doubt whether that part of your manuscript will ever see the light of day again."

Mitch spoke up. "Just how valuable do you think your manuscript is, Al?"

"That remains to be determined. No forensic analysis has been made yet. That was to be my next step."

"Exactly the next step I would propose," Drake agreed. "And I have the name and address of just such an analyst—Dr. Bernard Horne."

"Where'd you get that name, Sherman?"

"From the telephone book."

"What a scholar you are, Sherman! You want to take this potentially very valuable manuscript—or what's left of it—to the first guy you find in the Yellow Pages? How do you know he's any good?"

"Okay, Al, you're right. What we need to do is to get the names of several forensic analysts, check out their reputations as best we can, and then choose one."

"I agree. That's what we should do," Potter added.

Al raised his voice. "Where do you get that 'we' stuff? The manuscript is mine. What makes you think I want you clowns involved in any way? Haven't you done enough damage already?"

Drake responded humbly, "You're absolutely right, Al. We have no right to be involved. I know my stupidity has possibly caused you considerable loss. But I want to do what I can to compensate for my mistake. I'd like to do the legwork in looking for the right analyst. Then I'd like to share what I've learned with you. Of course, you'll be the one to select the analyst, but I'd like to help you by supplying the relevant information about your possible choices. Does that make sense?"

Trask reflected for a few seconds. "Yeah, I guess that'd be a start. I really want to find out the worth of what's left of my manuscript."

Potter joined in. "Al, you know I work in a bookstore. Maybe my boss could help us; he sometimes deals with rare books."

"That's probably a good place for you to start, Sherman," Trask suggested. "But the sticking point, as I see it, is how any of us or all of us can pay the analyst's fee?"

Drake responded, "Lawyers sometimes take a case on a contingency basis. Is that something you'd be willing to consider, Al?"

"If that's the only way we can get the job done, I suppose I have no choice. Yes, let's look into that possibility. As you contact your possible analysts, try that idea out on them, Sherman."

After a few more minutes of discussion, Potter and Drake left Trask's apartment. On the way home they agreed that Sherman should come to the bookstore right after work the next day, Tuesday. He could be there by six—Mitchell's boss wouldn't close the store until seven.

During the day, Mitch would seek his boss's advice about an analyst. Tuesday evening at 5:45, Drake entered Harry's Bookstore—one of the very few remaining non-chain bookstores. Harry Barnett, the owner, and Mitch were waiting.

After they went over the problem with him, Barnett advised, "Getting a list of people in that line of work is no problem. Picking out the best qualified may be something else."

After about thirty minutes Drake had his list with Harry's ratings, from one to ten, marked in pencil. Dr. Bernard Horne was rated a ten, a fact that pleased Drake.

Early in the evening, Drake called Trask with that information.

"Why don't you start with this Horne guy, Sherm?" suggested Trask. "If he looks legit, has the proper diplomas on his office wall, and if he'll work on contingency, let's go with him and not bother about the others."

"Sounds good to me, Al."

CHAPTER THIRTY-TWO

ELDER EDWARD HAYES

Edward Hayes and his wife, Stephanie, always enjoyed and appreciated the rare opportunity to visit any of their children or grandchildren scattered across the United States. They were especially delighted to visit their only son, Edward Junior, his wife, Nancy, and their three growing children. Sunday, May 17th, had been very enjoyable.

Monday had been another matter. The board of the insurance company, on which Hayes had once sat, had been in turmoil. He had been asked to serve as arbiter between two factions. One faction wanted to fire the CEO; the other wanted to give him a vote of confidence and a raise. Ed Hayes wasn't certain where he stood because he had not followed the affairs of the corporation since his call as an apostle. The two factions on the board had fought to a draw—even with Hayes's help— and the decision to fire or praise and raise the CEO had been put off for another month.

Now, on Tuesday afternoon, comfortably seated next to Stephanie in the first-class section of a giant airliner, Hayes was hoping his brethren in Salt Lake were unaware of his consulting. Perhaps the problem on the board could be broken down into more manageable units during the next month. Meanwhile, there was that troubling document. He recalled his conversation with Garth Garrick when the latter had informed him of the existence of the manuscript. He had known the document must be false—or had he?

I just hope that no one in Security has done anything foolish, he thought. *How would I handle the situation if I were the president of the quorum instead of the acting president? How would I handle it if I were in Tony Ririe's or Hank Cannon's shoes? Well, I think the situation calls for strong and direct action, but I'm not sure the others would agree.*

Stephanie was aware of his absorption in a knotty problem because he didn't engage any of the other passengers, as was his custom. Usually, he liked to lead an unsuspecting fellow-passenger into a discussion of the restored gospel—a practice that some of his seatmates enjoyed but which made enemies of others. Nor did he joke with the flight attendants. He didn't even take advantage of the technology in front of him to check on the status of his stocks. Stephanie was about to ask her husband what was bothering him but thought better of it.

Their usual Church Security driver met them as they deplaned, took their baggage stubs, and headed for the baggage pick-up area. Ed and Stephanie Hayes followed more slowly, knowing the time it takes for baggage to be available, even in a highly automated system.

In the car on their way home, their driver delivered his message: "President Ririe wants you to call him at home tonight before you turn in."

Ed Hayes felt a chill. His heart started to race. His palms became sweaty, but he tried to remain calm and rational. *Probably something to do with President Wood or President Lund*, he thought. *Don't worry until you find out more.*

He methodically went through his post-trip chores, then telephoned Ririe at his home.

"President, this is Ed. I have a message to call you."

"Yes, Ed. Did you have a good trip?"

"Excellent. Good visit with our son and his wife and kids. How're things on the home front?"

President Ririe responded slowly and deliberately. "Ed, something has come up which is quite troubling. There's no change in the condition of either President Wood or President Lund. But President Lund has asked for a meeting with you, Hank Cannon, and me at his home at ten o'clock tomorrow morning. Do you have anything on your schedule that would interfere?"

"No, I was just going to spend the morning taking care of accumulated correspondence. Can I pick you up or would you prefer to meet at President Lund's home?"

"Let's meet there, Ed. Hank'll ride up with me. See you then."

Ed Hayes was about to ask about the agenda but Ririe had already hung up. *I'll bet it's about that manuscript*, he concluded. He slept very poorly, even with the help of a pill and his blood pressure medicine.

Before retiring, Ririe called both Cannon and Belnap and asked to meet with them early the next morning in his office.

CHAPTER THIRTY-THREE

FORENSIC ANALYSIS

Drake met with Dr. Bernard Horne two days after Trask agreed on his name. Horne's walls were decorated with what Drake considered to be legitimate and appropriate diplomas and licenses. He informed Horne about the nature of the document, the missing pages, and the hopes Drake had for the remainder.

Initially, Horne was not receptive to the contingency fee idea. But after some consideration of the possible value of the document and what his proposed share of the selling price would amount to, he agreed—with one stipulation.

"If the document proves to be a forgery, I must recoup my out-of-pocket expenses. I would guess they could run as high as a thousand dollars."

Drake reluctantly agreed.

"When do I get to see this mysterious document, Mr. Drake?"

"Dr. Horne, I'll tell Al Trask about our conversation and find out whether he wants me to bring it to you or to bring it himself. I think we could have it to you within a very few days. As soon as I find out what Al wants to do, one of us will call for an appointment. Does that sound okay?"

"Yes, that'll be fine, but all three of you should be here. I'll need to acquaint you with the various methods I'll use to test the authenticity of that document."

"Do you have any idea about how much time it'll take to do the job?"

"Probably about two months."

On Monday evening, 25 May 2020, Drake, Potter, and Trask met by appointment in Horne's office. After introductions, Trask opened his briefcase and withdrew a carefully wrapped set of papers.

"So this is the mysterious document!" Horne exclaimed.

"Well, part of it. I thought this part would be sufficient for your tests, but I have more at home." Trask's comment raised three sets of eyebrows.

Horne asked, "How many pages do you have altogether and how many did you bring?"

"I have 55 pages here," responded Trask "There are about that many more at my home. Will that present a problem for you, Dr. Horne?"

"I can get a good start on what you've brought with you. If I need more, I'll call you."

Drake asked, "Can you give us some idea of the approaches you'll take as you examine this document, Dr. Horne?"

"Yes, I can. And these approaches are fairly standard procedure in my line of work. The first thing I usually do is called provenance. I would talk with Mr. Trask about how he got this material, how long he's had it, and where it's been in prior years.

"Then I'd examine the paper. Papermaking is a science with a very long history. Changes in the way paper's made have rather definite dates. I'd examine a sample taken from one page chosen at random and look at it under a microscope. The materials used in paper making have unique characteristics. Rag content helps to fix the date of manufacture of some papers. A mix of rags and fiber sets a later date—and so on. I'd also look for any evidence that the paper has been aged artificially."

He continued. "Ink would be the next thing. Certain kinds

of ink used in forgeries leave telltale signs. I'll look for those signs. Also, getting back to the paper, I'll look for evidence that the ink has bled through to the opposite side of the page. I'll also look to see if the bleeding of the ink on the written side is all in one direction. All ink spreads out just a little, noticeable under the microscope. If the bleeding is in one direction only, that's evidence the paper has been treated, probably with hydrogen peroxide or ammonium hydroxide or both."

He paused. They nodded their comprehension, and he summarized, "Well, there's more, such as ink solubility and brown stain under the ink of genuinely old documents. But that gives you an idea. To minimize costs, I'll examine your document between some bigger cases I'm currently handling. Any questions?"

Both Drake and Potter expected Trask to respond. When he didn't, Drake observed, "Seems rather complete to me, Dr. Horne. And you say it'll take about two months?"

"Yes. I'll call Mr. Trask when I've completed the job. If I find something that definitely proves this manuscript is a forgery, I'll let him know immediately. Otherwise, you can expect to hear from me in about two months."

The three visitors left Horne's office and went their separate ways. Trask, however, returned to Dr. Bernard Horne's office within the hour and had an earnest private conversation with him.

CHAPTER THIRTY-FOUR

PREEMPTIVE STRIKE COMMITTEE

Wednesday, 20 May 2020

When Cannon and Belnap were seated in Ririe's office, Ririe got right to the point—a point he had been considering privately for several days.

"Brethren, each of you told me something when I first introduced you to the manuscript—something that has troubled me increasingly ever since. I need to discuss that something with you now."

Cannon and Belnap looked at each other with raised eyebrows.

"Grant, you asked, 'What if the document proves to be genuine?' Hank, you said, 'Yes, but . . .'" And Ririe paused. "Am I quoting or paraphrasing each of you correctly?"

Two heads nodded affirmatively. "And, Grant, you asserted, 'We must have a valid, believable, acceptable plan of action ready to limit the damage.'"

Grant nodded again. Then Ririe continued. "Would I be correct in assuming that both of you would recommend that we take steps now in order to be prepared just in case this manuscript proves to have some merit? You first, Hank."

"Your assumption is correct," Hank responded.

"And you, Grant?"

"Yes, Tony, that is what I tried to convey to you several days ago," Grant answered.

"As certain as I am that the document is false, I've been thinking along those lines. Do you both still feel there is need to start preparation now should the worst happen? To act now rather than react later?"

Again a double silent assent.

"In that case, would you consider preparing a scenario detailing what the Church could or should do if and when we are convinced there is some validity to the claims Drake makes for the manuscript? Would the two of you accept that joint assignment?"

"I'd enjoy working closely with Grant, even on such an unpleasant task," Cannon replied.

"And I feel the same. I imagine that there would have to be some sort of position paper. If so, how would we get it in proper shape without involving our secretaries or others?"

"Yes, you probably will need some help with the write-up of your recommendations. I agree that it wouldn't be wise to use your own office staff for such a purpose."

Hank and Grant looked at each other as each shook his head in agreement. Grant waited for Hank to speak first. When Hank remained silent, Grant asked, "Does Marybeth have the necessary skills to do that job?"

"Yes, she does. She really knows how to make her word processor do her bidding. And that's what I was about to recommend. Hank, your reactions?"

"Perfect choice. She already knows about the manuscript, so no additional person will need to be brought into the inner circle."

"I'll find out how Marybeth would feel about such a request when I go home tonight," Ririe responded. "Just in case there's any more phone bugging, I'll call you at your homes when I get her response and just tell you that the typist is willing or is reluctant, as the case may be. Okay? Whether or not you involve Marybeth beyond the typing will be up to the two of you."

They also agreed that at some time in the future, depending on the proven validity of the manuscript, an announcement might need to be made to the church and to the public. Ririe observed, "That will probably be my job—a task I'll perform only after consultation with the two of you, with Marybeth, and with the Twelve."

They talked further about how to get their copy to Marybeth and how to receive her suggested revisions. They also considered how the rest of the Twelve would react if and when they learned that they hadn't been included from the beginning.

Tony made arrangements to visit with Joseph Lund on his way home. Lund was agreeable to the plans his three brethren were making.

At home that night, Tony broached the matter to Marybeth. "Although I'm convinced the manuscript we talked about this morning is a phony, Hank and Grant are not so sure. I've agreed to their separate suggestions that we need to take some steps now just in case there is any validity to that document."

"Why are you sharing this with me now?"

"Because Hank, Grant, and I want you to be the scribe, maybe help edit what they produce."

Marybeth was stunned. "All the wives of the leaders have been kept in the dark about the inner workings of the Church for generations. Now, it seems I am to be brought, partway at least, into the circle. Is that a wise move, Tony?"

Tony chuckled. "Maybe that's why the sisters have been kept at bay—you would question every move your husbands proposed."

Marybeth frowned, bowed low, then smiled broadly. "Tony, I know this is an important departure from the norm, made necessary by the conditions. Of course I'll do whatever you want me to do. Probably have to dust off my old *Strunk and White*."

"Your what?"

"*Strunk and White, The Elements of Style*, from my university days."

Over the next several weeks, Cannon and Belnap tried their skill at composing a statement. Marybeth, who was almost reluctant to accept the task initially, did more than merely put their hand-written notes on her word-processor—she reworked their drafts with the heartless red pencil of a professional editor. As time went by the three of them decided that their little group should have a name. They tried, 'Beat 'em to the Punch Committee.' Then 'Get There Firstest with the Mostest Committee.' Wisely, they decided on the more dignified 'Preemptive Strike Committee.'

How to begin their statement proved to be the sticking point. They tried, "It has come to the attention of the leaders of the Church that a document exists which purports to invalidate Joseph Smith's account of how the Book of Mormon, as we have it, came into being." Not direct enough. "The leaders of the Church of Jesus Christ of Latter-day Saints have become aware of a document which invalidates Joseph Smith's account of the coming forth of the Book of Mormon." Too direct, they decided. And so the struggle went on for several weeks. At one time, Cannon wanted to forget the whole task.

"The more I try to wrap myself around this whole thing, the more I feel like I'm trying to stop an atomic reaction that has already started," Cannon told the other two.

But Belnap and Marybeth wanted to keep trying and they convinced Cannon to "Hang in there!" And keep trying they did.

When Cannon and Belnap met with Ririe in his office from time to time, they discussed the possible results of such a new 'revelation.'

"Will we lose thousands, if not hundreds of thousands, of members?"

"Probably, but won't their numbers come from among the less active?"

"How much will the tithing receipts go down?"

"Probably plummet. But do the less active pay tithing?"

"Will we be able to keep all of the temples open?"

"Will we be financially able to run BYU and its satellite schools if the tithing receipts do indeed drop substantially?"

"Will we be able to support all of the mission offices, world-wide?"

"Will we have the missionaries needed to staff those offices?"

"How will I bear my testimony?"

"Can't we just say the gospel of Jesus Christ is still true?"

These and other pertinent questions were analyzed, discussed, and probed—but with no thoroughly satisfying answers.

They discussed when and how a Church statement would be made. They came to realize that if the Church took a stand on the document before it was presented to the world by its owners, they would be saying, "There is some validity to that document." However, if they waited until the anti-Mormon document was released, they wouldn't "beat 'em to the punch," but they would have their responses ready with little or no lead-time necessary.

And Cannon paraphrased for his two brethren what he had said to Marybeth and Grant earlier: "How can we stop an atomic reaction once it has been set in motion?"

Hearts were heavy.

CHAPTER THIRTY-FIVE

SON OF OBITUARY

The two cars carrying the three Church leaders—Ririe, Cannon, and Hayes—arrived at Lund's home on Wednesday, May 10th, at about the same time, each driven by a Church Security driver. Ed Hayes was startled to see Anthony Ririe's driver, Garth Garrick. He knew that for years Ririe had refused a driver, and now he had the top security man.

They told their drivers to go back to headquarters until they were called. After shaking hands warmly, they walked together in solemn silence to the front door, which Margaret promptly opened.

"Dad's in his den, Brethren. But before you go in, I think you might get a kick out of a conversation Dad and I had just before you arrived. I was looking over the morning paper when Dad asked me what section I was reading. When I told him I was reading the obits, he asked if his name was there. When I answered, 'No, of course not,' he responded with, 'Son-of-obituary!'"

"Certainly hasn't lost his sense of humor," Ririe observed. Nods of assent came from the others, but no smiles, which puzzled Margaret.

"Please go right in. If you need me for anything, I'll be doing genealogy in my den."

Despite Margaret's anecdote, not one of the three men had anything but trepidation in his heart. Ririe disliked confrontation of any sort; Cannon, who usually thrived on confrontation, this day was quite concerned; and Hayes hated to be confronted on anything. He felt that something unpleasant was coming—the earlier presence of Garth Garrick troubled him.

Tony Ririe motioned to Joseph Lund. "Please don't get up, President. It's good to see you looking so well."

"Yes, you're looking better than I've seen you for several weeks, President," Ed Hayes commented.

A smile flickered across Lund's face. He was thinking that Hayes had not come to visit him for several months. Hayes caught that smile and felt even more uncomfortable.

Lund motioned for the three men to be seated. "Why don't you sit here, Ed, and you, Hank, next to him? Tony, that ought to be your chair." He pointed to a seat next to a tape player that Hayes noticed for the first time.

President Lund began at once. "Tony, because most of what I know about this matter I've learned from you, why don't you fill in the details for Ed?"

Tony Ririe had told the story several times now and recounted it methodically in chronological order. Beginning with the preceding Monday, May 11th, he told of the call from Bishop Donavan, his meeting with him, seeing the manuscript and obtaining half of it, Grant Belnap's call from Harriet Hudson, his discovery of Garth Garrick's involvement, and Garrick's assertion that Hayes had ordered him to place the taps and steal the document. Ririe also told Hayes about the call from the Salt Lake Police Department. He recounted how he had counseled with Grant Belnap, had informed Henry Cannon at the earliest opportunity, and of the decisions about this meeting.

Hayes sat in complete silence until Ririe had finished.

Lund spoke again. "Tony, Hank, and I have agreed—no, we have insisted—that you, Ed, should be given every opportunity to rebut anything that has just been discussed before we decide if this matter should go before the full Twelve." Tony and Hank nodded.

Hayes tried to clear his throat but without much success before he responded, "Brethren, I deny being involved in this sordid affair in any way." Then he looked again at the tape recorder. "Please let me withdraw that statement, President Lund. I presume this tape will involve me in some way. Shall we hear it?"

Hear it they did.

I want surveillance in Grant Belnap's home . . . We have to protect him from himself . . . That manuscript must be in our hands . . . Garth, that's your job. Similar statements, as they had the first time he listened to the tape, brought tears to Lund's eyes. Ririe and Cannon were also teary-eyed. Only Hayes had dry eyes—eyes that appeared to bulge a little more as the words issued from the tape.

"Ed, my beloved brother in the Quorum, can you help us understand why you did what you did?" President Lund asked with great sincerity.

"I admit to knowing about the listening devices, but I didn't *order* them. And I categorically deny that I ordered Garth Garrick to steal that manuscript!"

"Let's look at them one at a time—the listening devices, then the alleged order to steal the manuscript. Are the words we just heard you utter regarding the listening devices of such a nature as to require that the matter come before the entire Quorum?" Lund asked.

Instead of answering the question, Hayes declared, "I need to take one of my tablets—probably just some angina I get every now and then." With that he placed a nitroglycerin tablet under his tongue.

This momentary diversion gave Hayes a few seconds to weigh his words—words that could determine his place in the Quorum, affect his status with the Lord in the hereafter, and possibly have a crushing effect on his wife and family.

"Brethren, as I just admitted, I unwisely agreed to the taps when Brother Garrick and I discussed them. But I did *not* order Garrick to steal the manuscript. That part of the tape we just heard has been doctored. I ask your forgiveness for my involvement in the taps. I'll also ask for Grant Belnap's forgiveness, as well. I hope with all my heart that this matter won't need to be known by my brethren in the Twelve."

"I understand your feelings, Ed. I, too, hope it won't be necessary for the matter of the taps to go beyond this room." President Lund spoke slowly and softly. "But I cannot ignore the words I just heard—your voice on the tape ordering the commission of a felony. The Church has learned over the years that hiding a mistake is a greater mistake. Tony, Hank, what are your individual recommendations?"

Ririe spoke first. "Brethren, in the absence of President Wood, I feel we have no option but to put the entire matter before the Quorum, with you, President Lund, presiding."

"Hank?" Lund nodded to the other counselor.

"There is absolutely no doubt in my mind: This matter must come before the entire quorum tomorrow, Thursday!" Hank Cannon did not surprise Tony with his forcefulness. Lund and Hayes, on the other hand, were somewhat taken aback.

"Hank, why do you think this step should take place so precipitously?" Hayes asked.

"I'll tell you why, Ed. Because the enemies of the Church could create all kinds of mischief if we don't take corrective action before the mess comes out. And believe me, Brethren, some parts of it—if not all—will eventually become public."

Tony, fully aware of the ethical as well as legal necessity of returning the document to its owner, was just about to ask Hayes its location when he noticed that Hayes was close to collapse. Ririe and Cannon helped him to the couch.

"Tony," Lund shouted, "Call 911. Then call Sister Hayes and tell her Ed is not well. Margaret, please bring a damp cloth."

Hayes was not feigning, but he was not unconscious. "Brethren, I swear that tape has been doctored. But, please give me a blessing," he pleaded as Margaret placed the cool cloth on his forehead. "Never mind the oil. Lay your hands on my head and, by the power of your priesthood and your callings, bless me to survive. But if this matter must go before the Twelve, bless me to die." With that Edward Hayes lost consciousness.

Lund asked the other two men to give Hayes a blessing to recover and to be equal to whatever the future might hold. This they completed just before the ambulance arrived.

The emergency medical team soon determined that their patient had a pulse, albeit weak, and symptoms of a coronary occlusion. They recommended that he be transported to the hospital immediately.

"Hank, maybe you should ride with Ed to the hospital," Ririe whispered to President Cannon. "Make sure he doesn't say anything he shouldn't."

The team took their patient gently to the waiting ambulance and, with Hank Cannon aboard, sped toward the LDS Hospital, just a few blocks away.

"Tony, were you able to reach Sister Hayes?"

"Yes, Joseph. I talked with her all the time the ambulance people were here. She's now on her way to the hospital in her own car; she didn't want to wait for a church driver."

"Thanks, Tony. This isn't exactly the way I thought our meeting would end."

CHAPTER THIRTY-SIX

SAVING A REPUTATION

Margaret went into her computer room; Lund and Ririe were left to think about what had just transpired. Lund spoke first.

"Maybe the Lord is saving Ed Hayes's reputation in the eyes of the world, Tony, although I'm not certain just how directly He interferes with the normal processes of life and disease. But what about his assertion the tape was doctored? Could that be true?"

"I'm worried about that assertion, but I agree with you on both of your other points. Looking at it from the view of Ed and his family, if he died now, his involvement in this mess may never need to be made public. However, if he does recover, can he be allowed to continue as a member of the Twelve?"

"Let's wait until we learn what his condition is and what the medical prognosis turns out to be," Lund replied. "But I want you to follow up on Ed's claim that the tapes have been doctored. That means you should keep them in your personal possession."

"I'll do that."

They continued to discuss the events of recent days, including Hayes's serving as a consultant contrary to very specific church policy prohibiting such activities for General Authorities.

"Tony," Lund asked, his voice weak, "would you please have Margaret help me to my room? The events of the last few minutes have hit me hard."

Ririe immediately went for Margaret, and the two of them

assisted the feeble ninety-year-old president of the quorum to his room. Margaret removed her father's shoes, massaged his feet briefly, and then covered him with the ever-present afghan robe.

"Tony, why don't you go back to your office?" Lund suggested. "If we get any word from the hospital, we'll let you know. Better still, why don't you call the emergency room and talk to Hank. Tell him our meeting here is over for the day and that you're going back to your office. He'll keep both of us informed."

Tony Ririe made two phone calls: one for Garth Garrick to pick him up and the other to the ER and Hank Cannon.

After seeing that her father was comfortably settled, Margaret left his room and rejoined Ririe.

"I sincerely hope Elder Hayes's problem isn't serious," Margaret said anxiously.

"And I do, too. But more than that, I hope Elder Hayes's collapse hasn't been too hard on your father."

"One of Dad's favorite statements is, 'I'm a tough old bird.' And he is."

"Margaret, I feel I must tell you, but in the strictest confidence, that the matters we were discussing just before Elder Hayes collapsed were very distressing to all of us. I think that's what caused his collapse. I just hope your father hasn't been hit by those matters as hard as Elder Hayes has."

They chatted for a few more moments, then both the phone and the doorbell rang at the same time.

"I'll get the door if you'll get the phone," Ririe suggested. He let Garth Garrick in and explained the absence of the others.

"President Ririe, it's for you. From the sound of President Cannon's voice, I don't think he has good news."

"Thank you, Margaret. Yes, Hank."

"It's over, Tony. They're still working on him, but all indications are that he had a massive coronary."

"Is his wife there yet?" Ririe asked.

"She's just walking in the door. I better hang up so I can be with her."

Turning to Margaret and Garrick as he hung up the telephone, Ririe told them, "Elder Hayes appears to have been dead on arrival."

"That is bad news," Margaret observed feelingly.

But both Ririe and Garrick had a different fleeting thought.

"Margaret, why don't you quietly take a peek at your father?" Ririe's voice was subdued. "If he's asleep, I don't want to wake him. But if he's awake, then perhaps I should break the news to him."

Margaret found her father sitting up with his telephone receiver on his lap.

"President Ririe," Margaret called from the bedroom door, "he's awake. He was listening on his extension. Why don't you come in?"

When he entered, Margaret positioned a chair for Ririe next to the bed and then excused herself. She went out to give Garrick more details about Elder Hayes's collapse and the arrival of the ambulance. She thought Garrick looked more distressed now than any of the others had been when Hayes was taken away by ambulance.

CHAPTER THIRTY-SEVEN

STEPHANIE HAYES

Stephanie Hayes was a strong woman. After she got over the initial shock of hearing what Hank Cannon had to say about her husband's collapse, of seeing him on the table attached to myriad wires and tubing, and observing all the activities of the four ER nurses and doctor who were still trying to revive him, she turned to the MD.

"Is he clinically dead?" she asked.

"Yes, Mrs. Hayes, he's clinically dead. The ambulance people told me they thought he was dead on arrival."

"Then why are you still working on him?"

"We've been able to revive some people in situations like this."

Stephanie asked quietly, "How long has his brain been without oxygen?"

He glanced at his watch. "Even though we immediately put him on a ventilator, it's been about half an hour." He looked at her calm face and continued. "I'm afraid there's irreparable damage to his central nervous system."

"Was it a coronary or a cerebral aneurysm?"

"A massive coronary."

Stephanie closed her eyes for a moment; but when she spoke, it was without a tremor. "Thank you, doctor. My husband's wishes—which are in writing with a copy in this hospital—are that you cease all efforts to revive him. Those are my wishes as well."

"You are a very brave and wise person, Mrs. Hayes." Turning to his team, the doctor ordered, "Remove the equipment. Cover him except for his head. Then let's give Mrs. Hayes some privacy."

Hank Cannon, who had been standing in the background, moved toward Stephanie Hayes. "Should I stay or would you prefer to be alone?"

"Hank, please stay."

Stephanie walked to the gurney, kissed her husband's barely warm lips, and then turned to Hank Cannon. "Let's find some privacy, Hank. I need help with the next steps."

A sympathetic nurse led them to a small consultation room down the hall where they took chairs facing each other. Two table lamps in diagonally opposite corners provided soothing light for the quiet decor. A telephone was located by one of the lamps.

"Hank, this is what I think I must do today. Please take notes for me so I won't forget anything."

Cannon took out his pen and a blank three-by-five card he always carried in his shirt pocket. He was thinking, *Why isn't she in tears? How can she be in such total control of herself?*

"Ed and I have arrangements with the McHenry Mortuary, but they'll need to be notified. Would you do that for me, Hank?"

"Yes, just as soon as you are prepared to leave."

"I must notify the children. I can do that from home. What about the Church press people? When will they want to release a statement?"

"Our press people always want to get such news out at the earliest possible moment, but we can insist that they hold off until tomorrow morning, if you prefer. But you shouldn't be alone right now."

"My daughter, Kathleen, lives just down the street from me. Would you please call her? Just tell her that I'm not feeling well and that I'd like to have her in my home when I arrive. Here's her number."

Cannon made the call from the nearby telephone.

"Word of Ed's death will already be in the grapevine through the hospital and ambulance personnel," he pointed out. "If you like, right after I call the mortuary, I'll notify the Church's Public Relations office. They can give you an hour—more if you prefer—to notify your immediate family. Unfortunately, some of your relatives will learn of Ed's death through the press, but I don't see how that can be prevented entirely."

Stephanie nodded. "I understand." She continued, collectedly, to dictate a list of "to do" items.

"Would you drive me home, Hank? My car's in the parking lot. Call your driver before we leave the hospital, and he can pick you up at my house."

"There's the funeral, Stephanie, but the General Authority Committee will want to wait until your children can be here. Tomorrow or tomorrow night will be fine."

"Maybe we can discuss my preferences in the car, Hank. I'd prefer that to idle chitchat. And I don't want you telling me what a great man Ed was. I know his strengths and weaknesses better than anyone."

As Henry Cannon, Second Counselor in the First Presidency, drove the widow of one of the senior apostles home, they discussed her husband's funeral. The wishes of the family would take second place to the protocol in such cases. The family's preferences for music would be honored but the committee would determine the balance of the services. General Authorities rather than her local bishop would be in charge. Music by the Tabernacle Choir, of course. All the while, part of Hank Cannon's mind worried about what tongues would wag if anyone recognized him driving with a woman who was not his wife. And another part thought about Stephanie Hayes's composure. *How does she do it?* Cannon wondered.

When Cannon parked Stephanie's car in the Hayes's driveway, he saw Kathleen at the door. His own car and driver were waiting at the curb.

Hank Cannon escorted Stephanie Hayes to the front door and whispered to Kathleen, "Your mother has just had a great shock that she'll tell you about. Do you want me to stay, Stephanie?"

He was relieved when she responded, "No, but thank you, Hank. I don't know what I'd have done without you."

"May the Lord bless you both." And Cannon turned toward his car. He mentally followed mother and daughter into the house where the tears, the previously absent tears, finally let loose. He knew that the balance of their day would be consumed in telephone calls to shocked children and other relatives.

CHAPTER THIRTY-EIGHT

GETTING THE WORD OUT

From his cell phone, Cannon called the McHenry Mortuary, only to learn they had been informed by the hospital and would pick up the body as soon as it was released.

Cannon then called Joseph Lund to confirm that Hayes was dead. The next call was to Ririe's office.

"Hank, where are you?" came Ririe's voice

"I'm in my car returning to your office. Should be there in less than fifteen minutes barring traffic delays."

"Anything we should discuss now?"

"No. It was a coronary, and Stephanie ordered life support turned off as she and Ed had previously decided. I believe anything else I have to say can wait."

In the rear-view mirror Cannon saw his driver's expression—a cross between a grimace and a smile. *Is he one of Hayes's key men in the Church Security Department?* He was glad he'd decided to say nothing.

Cannon went directly to Ririe's office, where he gave the senior counselor a detailed account of everything he'd done since leaving with the ambulance.

After taking in Cannon's report, Ririe responded, "Thanks, Hank. I've talked with our press people, and they're preparing a release to go out ASAP. I don't want the TV stations in town saying anything about Ed Hayes's death before our official release. Any ideas?"

Cannon, in his usual manner, was not slow to respond. "Tony, shouldn't that release go out immediately? I told Stephanie we'd hold the release long enough for her to notify her immediate family before they learned the news from the media. It's now about 12:30. Would a four o'clock release give Sister Hayes enough time?"

"I think so, but why don't you try to reach her and see how she feels about that release time. Then give me the phone so I can express my condolences. "

This was done.

"Hank, one more thing. The tapes. Both Joseph Lund and I have uneasy feelings about their accuracy, their truthfulness. Joseph told me to safeguard them. Before you came in, I called Margaret and asked her to lock the recorder and tapes in a closet until I can pick them up personally."

"Wise move, Tony, and I share your concerns about what's on those tapes. As I listened, I thought I heard too many breaks. An electronics expert could check that. Hey, one of the stake presidents at the Denver Area Conference does that for a living. What do you think? Shall I contact him?"

And so the wheels were set in motion for President Ross Bingham to evaluate the tapes.

"I hate to be mundane at a time like this, Tony, but I'm hungry," confessed Cannon. "Have you eaten yet?"

"Not yet. Good idea. Let's go."

In the General Authorities' dining room, they found clusters of priesthood leaders conversing in hushed tones

All eyes turned toward Ririe, and he realized he needed to make an announcement. "Folks, could I have a word?" An immediate hush settled over the room. "Yes, it's true. We lost Ed Hayes an hour or so ago. Massive coronary. We want to keep it out of the media as long as possible. That will give Sister Hayes time to notify her immediate family." Ririe paused briefly while he considered how much to say.

"Elder Hayes was meeting with President Lund, President Cannon, and me at President Lund's home when he experienced some angina. He put a nitroglycerin tablet under his tongue, then collapsed. President Cannon and I gave him a blessing while we were waiting for the ambulance to arrive. President Cannon rode with him in the ambulance. He apparently expired in the ambulance and was pronounced dead at LDS Hospital after the ER personnel had done their utmost to revive him. Sister Hayes arrived at the hospital only moments after the ambulance and confirmed that he would not want continued life support given his condition. Now, I must ask you, and you sisters behind the counter as well, not to discuss Elder Hayes's death with anyone outside this room until the official press release has been issued."

With that, the two counselors picked up their trays, selected their lunches, and headed for a corner table. The room, never noisy, was considerably more quiet than usual.

CHAPTER THIRTY-NINE

ED HAYES'S FUNERAL

At the Hayes's home, Stephanie Hayes, with Kathleen's help, spent several hours calling her other four children, living all over the country, and other close relatives, on both sides of the family.

That night she found it necessary to switch on her answering machine as calls began flooding in immediately after the six o'clock news anchor announced, "This word from LDS Church headquarters: Elder Edward Hayes, a senior member of the Church's Quorum of the Twelve Apostles, collapsed and died of an apparent heart attack shortly before noon today. More details as they become available."

Although Stephanie was still shaken by her husband's death, she thought about how she'd like his funeral handled. She knew from past experience she would prefer to have Ed's services in the Tabernacle rather than in the much larger Hinckley Conference Center. The family would gather at the mortuary two hours before the service. There would be a family prayer, the final good-byes, the final adjustments of his temple robes, and the closing of the casket. The police would escort the cortege to the Tabernacle. She'd make the long walk behind the casket as her older grandsons carried it from a southwest entrance to the front row of that venerable building.

One of the Tabernacle organists would be playing a subdued prelude. At noon exactly, the presiding officer of the Church—most likely President Ririe—would stand and say something like, "We are here to pay our last earthly respects to one of the Lord's noble servants, Elder Edward Hayes."

The brief obituary would give his birth date, ?
parents. His ancestry, which dated back to the
of the Church, would be alluded to gracefully. F
unstacked in orderly events: his schooling, his career, and
church service which culminated in his calling to the Quorum
of the Twelve in 1995 followed by twenty-five years of faithful,
diligent, inspirational service.

The Tabernacle Choir would present moving and appropriate music drawn from the musical heritage of both the
Church and the world. Other speakers, chosen by the
committee, would discuss the plan of salvation, the reality of
life after death, the reunion with loved ones, and the promise
of family togetherness in the hereafter. She always had trouble
with the concept of a nuclear family—a mother, a father, and
their children enjoying eternity as one family. How would the
parents in that family relate to their own parents? And how
could the children simultaneously be with their own parents
when they would be parents to their own children? *Perhaps,
she thought, the family unit in the hereafter really will be just
husband and wife, with visitation privileges up and down the
family tree. But it was all in the hands of a kind and merciful
Father in Heaven, so why worry?*

After the benediction, probably by Ed's younger brother,
the cortege would drive to the city cemetery where they would
gather for the prayer dedicating the grave.

And then I will come back to my empty home, she thought.
It was orderly, ritualistic, smooth. As the widow she had a
clearly defined role to play. She would fulfill it to the letter, just
as she had fulfilled her other roles. It was easier to fit into that
role than to rethink a new one.

Over the next few days, the funeral arrangements were
made and carried out, almost exactly as she had supposed that
first night at home without Ed.

She would receive periodic calls and visits from Ed's brethren. They would diminish in frequency as Ed faded into history. She had heard one publisher of LDS books comment that there is nothing deader than a dead General Authority. "*Sic transit gloria mundi,*" she thought correctly.

Left alone, she tackled the task of disposing of her husband's personal effects with her usual energy and efficiency. Tony Ririe had made an odd request—would she watch for anything that appeared to be a very old manuscript?

She distributed cuff links, ties, and tie clips to the grandsons. To the granddaughters went Ed's books. She had Deseret Industries come and empty his clothes closet.

Then she started to go through his files, some of which had been delivered from church headquarters not long after his death.

One filing cabinet in Ed's home office had always been a bit of a mystery to Stephanie. It was always locked, and the drawers had no labels on them. It was a long time before she found the right key. When she did, she was startled at the drawers full of conspiracy theory literature and even correspondence her husband had accumulated.

She purchased a paper shredder.

CHAPTER FORTY

DEATH OF A PROPHET

President Anthony Ririe and President Henry Cannon spent the balance of May and all of June in routine matters. Ririe kept in touch with Bishop Donavan who continued his service to the members in his Salt Lake Diocese. Both were concerned and disappointed that no trace had yet been found of the missing manuscript.

Belnap, a more sprightly man since his mid-June proposal to Norma Ashcraft, carried out his assigned duties and traveled from time to time to huge regional conferences in all parts of the world. He and Norma selected a large apartment near church headquarters and furnished it with pieces from his house and from her apartment, including her complete home-office, and with other items they purchased together. Thus each had items to remind them of the past and new things to share as they created their future home.

In the Chicago area, life went on pretty much as usual for Sherman Drake, Mitchell Potter, Albert Trask, and Harriet Hudson, with one exception: Harriet's drinking. Ever since her ill-fated trip to Salt Lake City, her drinking had spiraled out of control. Drake told her she would kill herself if she didn't slow down. Her response: "How will that make any difference to anyone at all?"

The quality and quantity of her work suffered as well, resulting in her being warned by the senior partner: "Lay off or be laid off!"

One of President Ririe's weekly tasks, although he did not regard it as such, was to call on Joseph Lund. President Wood was no longer receiving visitors because he was in a coma and incapable of response. The family wanted his last days to be just with them, and Ririe thought that was the way it should be—the way he'd want it for himself.

Each time Ririe visited Lund, whose health slowly continued to fail, the latter would repeat his feeling that, if he survived President Wood, the Lord would not want him to assume the mantle of the Prophet. Each time, Ririe remonstrated, "Why don't we leave that up to the Lord, Joseph?"

Shortly after Elder Hayes's funeral, Ririe asked Lund when he was going to fill the vacancy in the Twelve.

"Given President Wood's condition," Lund responded, "and the fact that I am not the head of the Church, I prefer to wait for subsequent events before acting on that one."

"I think I understand, Joseph," Ririe assured him.

During Ririe's visit to Lund on Monday, June 29, they talked about the many worldwide events through which members of the Church would celebrate the arrival of the pioneers in the Salt Lake Valley. Lund was pleased with the reports but lamented his inability to attend any such activities.

Then Lund once again expressed his doubts about the succession, and Ririe once more gave his counter-argument. This time, however, Lund pressed the point. "Somebody has to change this custom of seniority succession. I want to go down in the history of the Church as the one who did just that, Tony."

Ririe answered with a mild suggestion of reproof. "The precedent of seniority succession has worked reasonably well for nearly two hundred years, Joseph. Do you want to change it just so you can go down in history as the one who did?"

"No, Tony. I worded that poorly. Doing it's the important thing, not how history'll treat me. I've seen too many counselors in the First Presidency struggle to lead the Church when their leader was completely incapacitated. I've made this a matter of serious thought and much prayer. If I outlive President Wood, I'll refuse to serve as his successor."

That resolve was soon tested. Just before the daily eight o'clock meeting of the First Presidency on Tuesday, June 30, Ririe received word that President James D. Wood, a man whom he sustained as a latter-day prophet, seer, and revelator, had died.

Ririe at once called Margaret Perry and asked if he and Hank Cannon could visit President Lund immediately. There they tactfully broke the news of Wood's death. It was not a surprise. After reminiscing for a few minutes about the long and fruitful career of their dear friend, they fell silent.

Ririe broke the silence. "President Lund, I know I don't have to tell you, but you now officially preside over the Church in your capacity as president of the quorum. How would you like us, President Wood's former counselors, to proceed?"

"Carry on, brethren, carry on," Lund responded without hesitation. "You know I can't come to the office or handle any of the day-to-day routine. Let's see—today's Tuesday. I think it would be inappropriate for the quorum to consider the new First Presidency before President Wood's funeral. That means the matter won't be considered by the Quorum until one week from Thursday."

"May I make a suggestion, President?"

Lund responded somewhat impatiently. "Tony, let's stick with first names, and, for heaven's sake, you don't have to ask me if you can make a suggestion."

"Joseph, I rather suspect that President Wood's funeral won't be held before Monday, July 6th, because of the Fourth of July holiday. Couldn't the Twelve meet in the temple the following Thursday?"

"Isn't that what I just said? Anyway, it sounds reasonable to me, Tony."

After only a few more minutes' discussion it was decided to hold the funeral on Monday, subject to family approval, of which they felt certain. The Twelve would reorganize the First Presidency at their regularly scheduled temple meeting on Thursday, July 9. In the meantime, the two counselors would continue to function as if nothing had changed.

"Hank," Lund asked, "would you see if you can get a member of President Wood's family on the line for me? I want to express my condolences. Then I want you and Tony to talk with them about funeral plans. If they're not ready to talk about those plans now, suggest that it be done tomorrow."

President Lund was soon telling President Wood's youngest son, himself sixty years old, how much he loved his father and how much he'd miss him.

Hank Cannon took the phone and, after condolences, asked if the family had made any preliminary plans for the funeral. He was surprised to learn that a fax had just been sent to President Ririe's office with a complete outline of the funeral, subject to the approval of the Brethren.

Lund surprised the two counselors again when he told them with mock gruffness, "I haven't had breakfast yet. Will you two get back to work so I can eat?"

Ririe spoke for both counselors when he declared, "We love you, Joseph. Stay well. You are needed."

Despite the levity of the remarks and the death of their dear colleague and friend, all three leaders continued to worry about the manuscript, its whereabouts and its potential validity.

In the Chicago area, Harriet Hudson read of the death of the President of the Church and wondered what that might mean to Grant Belnap. *For sure, he'll move up one chair in seniority.*

Drake also saw the announcement. *A different headman, but the impact of the manuscript will be the same.* Impatiently, he wondered how Horne was progressing with his analysis.

President Wood's funeral was held in much the same pattern as Edward Hayes's. The only differences were that it was held in the Hinckley Conference Center and the crowds were much larger. So was the police escort. The eulogy—delivered by President Cannon—catalogued Wood's long and dedicated service at several levels of the Church hierarchy, and noted its growth in terms of number of members, missionaries, and temples. More important than numbers, however, Hank Cannon stressed how President Wood had reached out to all, in and out of the Church, in love and kindness. He used some personal anecdotes to illustrate his points.

The sermons were theologically comforting. The speakers stressed the assurance of life after death, the divinity of the work, the sacred calling of Joseph Smith, and the truth of the Book of Mormon. The youngest son dedicated the grave. Movingly, he included the words, "Until we meet again, Dad."

The captains and the kings departed. Life went on.

As the two counselors in the former First Presidency held their daily meetings, as instructed by Joseph Lund, their only superior officer, they took special care to see that Grant Belnap received no assignments until the first week in September.

"That good man and his bride deserve time for a long honeymoon," Tony told Hank, who agreed wholeheartedly.

Subsequent events, however, delayed and shortened that honeymoon.

CHAPTER FORTY-ONE

"THUS SAYETH THE LORD"

Thursday, 9 July 2020

Three days after the funeral of President James D. Wood, the Quorum of the Twelve met in their council chamber in the Salt Lake Temple. Normally fifteen, their ranks now consisted of thirteen. Following long-standing custom, they held a prayer circle dressed in their temple robes, then changed to their street clothes and took their seats arranged around the room in the order of their seniority, with Ririe and Cannon assuming their positions in the quorum.

Then Joseph R. Lund, who had sat through several such meetings during his long life of service in the Church, reminded the others what most of them already knew. Starting with the most recently ordained apostle, each man in turn would present his views on who should be the next president. Each declared that Joseph R. Lund should assume the presidency and should choose his own counselors.

Then it was Lund's turn. The senior apostle in such cases always spoke last. Only Ririe and Cannon were prepared to hear what he told them.

"Brethren, since the days of Brigham Young, we have followed the procedure you recommend. Some have expressed the opinion that this procedure is doctrine. I think it's not doctrine but rather is a custom that's been given an exalted status because we've never departed from it."

He paused, then continued, his aged voice firm, "I've made what I just said, and what I'm about to say, a matter of serious prayer. I believe the Lord helps us find answers to questions we bring to him, but that he doesn't answer questions we don't ask. I've asked the Lord if I should succeed President Wood. The Lord's answer has come to me very clearly, 'No.'"

A murmur of shock and surprise ran around the room. "Now, I'd like to hear from each of you again," President Lund requested. "I want to know if you believe in prayer. I want to know if you believe God hears and answers our prayers. I want to know if you'll support me, the senior apostle, when I say, with respect to my not taking on the mantle of the prophet, 'Thus sayeth the Lord.'"

Absolute silence enveloped the room. No one stirred. No man looked to his associates sitting on either side of him.

"President Ririe, I'd like to hear from you first, then the others in order of seniority."

Ririe was not quite prepared for the statement, "Thus sayeth the Lord," but he attempted to express himself.

"Brethren, I love, honor, respect, and sustain Joseph Lund as the mouthpiece of the Lord," Ririe stated with firmness. "But what he's just proposed leaves me in a quandary. If we bypass the senior apostle, do we throw the selection open to any of us, or do we decide on the basis of seniority? One of the strongest arguments for following the traditional practice of choosing the senior apostle is that politicking for office is completely eliminated. Over the years we have avoided the situation in which the Catholic cardinals find themselves every time they meet to select a new Pope."

"Excuse me, Tony," Joseph Lund interrupted. "If this body sustains my statement, I, as the retiring President of the Quorum of the Twelve, will nominate the next man in seniority: you, Brother Ririe. That way we'd have the best of both approaches. Now, please go on."

Ririe paused, cleared his throat, then continued with some

difficulty, "I believe in prayer. I believe God hears and answers prayers. I have no doubt of President Lund's authority to say, 'Thus sayeth the Lord.' But I also believe in thoughtful consideration of the answers we receive. I believe that taking our time in this matter would be wise. For that reason, after each of the rest of you has spoken, I'll move to adjourn this meeting without a decision for one week. That'll give all of us time to ask the Lord individually our own questions in this matter, to reflect on the possible consequences of going in the direction President Lund tells us the Lord wants us to go. But let's hear from the rest of you."

Each apostle in turn then pretty much agreed with Anthony Ririe's view. Some added that the counselors to President Wood should continue to function in consultation with President Lund and the Twelve.

As each of his brethren had his say, Grant Belnap silently recalled something he had memorized years before, a quotation from Machiavelli: *And it ought to be remembered that there is nothing more difficult to take in hand, more perilous to conduct, or more uncertain in its success, than to take the lead in the introduction of a new order of things.*

When the junior man had spoken, Ririe made his motion, which Cannon seconded, and the vote was taken—unanimous in the affirmative.

"Brethren, I have spoken, and you have spoken," President Lund stated. "I think the Lord has spoken as well through this motion. After the benediction, let's go back to our duties, not utter a word about what's just transpired, and individually seek the inspiration of the Almighty as to what action we should take when we meet again. Elder Belnap, would you please offer a closing prayer?"

As they departed, most of the brethren were thinking only of what steps would be taken when they next met, but three of them were also still concerned about the potentially fateful missing document.

Secretaries in many offices wondered why their bosses had returned so early from a meeting they expected to last much longer. They all knew better than to ask. Rosalie Torres called Tony Ririe to find out what sort of a release Public Communications should prepare. She was startled to hear, "No release will be necessary."

Joseph Lund reached his home at 10 a.m.

"Dad, you're home sooner than I expected, and you look discouraged," Margaret exclaimed. "Anything special you want to talk about?"

"Nothing I can talk about. But no matter what symptoms you see in me, don't call the doctor."

Margaret got him to his bed, took off his coat, tie, and shoes, and covered him again with the familiar afghan. As she turned to leave the room, she heard her father say, "Man proposes, but God disposes." Then she heard him call out softly, "Joseph, Joseph, Joseph." When she reached his side, she knew he was dead. *Had he been welcomed to the other side by the Prophet Joseph Smith himself?* She was convinced such was the case.

Respecting her father's wishes, Margaret didn't call the doctor but sat by his side for a full hour. Then she telephoned President Ririe, who, with Hank Cannon, came immediately to the home.

"Come in, Brethren. Dad's resting peacefully now." And she told them of his last words. They, too, were convinced the Prophet of the Restoration had greeted him on the other side of the veil.

Margaret told them she could notify all of the necessary relatives within a matter of hours. Ririe called Rosalie Torres and suggested the release go out in time for the six o'clock news.

As they stepped off the Lund front porch, Ririe turned to Cannon and remarked, "When will the document mystery be resolved?"

Cannon responded with, "And in whose favor?"

CHAPTER FORTY-TWO

GARTH GARRICK

Thus, on Monday, July 13, another funeral was held in the Hinckley Conference Center. A sweet spirit of love and peace comforted the more than 20,000 mourners. Among the dignitaries were the governor and the mayor, neither of whom was a Mormon, Bishop Patrick Donavan, and the leaders of all of the other faiths in the greater community, Christian and non-Christian alike. The speeches were similar to those given at President Wood's funeral, including reference to President Lund's well-known reputation as an exemplar of the Savior's love. The music was moving. And members of the Salt Lake City Police Department respectfully escorted the cortege to the cemetery.

Shortly after Garth Garrick drove Ririe to his office from the cemetery, he phoned, his voice tense, "President Ririe, I need to see you as soon as possible about the missing manuscript."

Ririe told him to come right over.

Obviously distraught, Garrick entered Ririe's inner office, carrying a large brown envelope.

"Garth, please sit down before you fall down. You look ill or extremely agitated."

"I'm both, President, and with good reason. Here's the manuscript. Yes, I stole it, and I lied to you about it." He began to sob.

Ririe wasn't completely surprised by this confession because Sgt. Sorensen had informed him that, in his opinion, Orvil Collins, whom Garrick had asserted to be the culprit, was completely innocent.

"It must be very difficult for you to admit this, Garth. I admire your courage in owning to the truth so candidly."

"President, can I ever be forgiven for my actions? Will I be held accountable for the death of Elder Hayes?"

"Two very real and pertinent questions, Garth. We believe in a God not only of justice but also of mercy. My answer to both of your questions is that they are in the hands of the Lord who will judge justly and mercifully when you meet him face to face."

"Thank you, President Ririe. In the meantime, what's to become of me? Will criminal charges be filed?" His sobbing gradually subsided.

"That won't be up to me alone. The entire First Presidency eventually will need to discuss that at length. But my immediate reaction is that we must not hide your actions from the owners of the manuscript and the proper law enforcement agencies. The Church learned long ago not to do that."

"What about a disciplinary council?" Garrick asked.

"A very likely possibility," Ririe responded.

Ririe moved around his desk and took the chair next to Garth. Putting his arm around Garrick's shoulder, he reminded him that Christ died for our sins. *But is Garth a sorrowful sinner or a manipulator?* Ririe wondered.

"What about my position with Church Security?"

"Hank Cannon and I must discuss your position with Church Security and the status of your temple recommend. Does your wife know anything about this?"

"Yes, President. She's devastated, but she'll stand by me. By the way, I didn't tell her about the contents of the manuscript— just that I stole it."

"I'm glad to hear that, Garth. Let's keep it that way," Ririe replied. Then he queried, "Garth, what precipitated your confession? You've held it to yourself for several weeks."

"You did, President. In your most recent editorial in the *Ensign* you quoted Sir Walter Scott:

Oh, what a tangled web we weave,

When first we practice to deceive.

"Somehow that got to me. My tangled web was starting to choke me. I resisted it as long as I could. But standing in the throng around President Lund's gravesite—looking at all of the Lord's servants there—I thought of what would happen to me in heaven when my life is over."

"Thank you for sharing that with me, Garth. No, we won't be able to hide anything when we finally stand before the judgment seat. While the rest of your life will be colored by your unwise actions, you would've been much more miserable had you not had this conversation with me. You've just told me what caused you to confess. Can you tell me what moved you to steal that document?"

"Yes, President. I thought I was acting in the best interests of the Church by attempting to keep that document out of the hands of its rightful owners."

"In other words, you thought the document could be true and could cause irreparable harm to the Church and its members—is that right?"

"Right, President."

"One more question, Garth. Did you doctor the tapes to incriminate Elder Hayes?"

Garrick hung his head and responded almost inaudibly, "Yes, President, I did."

After some further sobbing, consoling and counseling, Garrick left his leader's office—never to return—a most dejected man.

CHAPTER FORTY-THREE

THE NEW PROPHET AT WORK

Ririe immediately telephoned Hank Cannon and Grant Belnap personally, asking them to drop everything and come to his office. Both arrived within minutes and were incredulous as they learned of the manuscript's reappearance and Garrick's confession.

"Brethren," President Ririe summarized, "what to do about Garth Garrick can wait. I have two questions for you. First, since Pat Donavan was involved in all this from the time Drake arrived in town, does he need to be involved at this point? Second, can we keep this document—the object of a police investigation—long enough to have our experts look at it more thoroughly?"

Cannon, as usual, was the first to respond. "Let's leave Bishop Donavan out of it for now. And, yes, let's keep the manuscript long enough for a thorough forensic analysis."

"Grant, your reactions, please."

"Tony, I can see where Hank's coming from with respect to Pat Donavan. But will your long and cherished friendship with him permit you to do that? After all, he's consistently been candid with you. Is it fair for you to conceal something like this from him? But I do agree with Hank on the matter of the forensic analysis."

"Although I felt the need to inform Pat Donavan at once," Ririe responded, "I wanted your counsel. But would it be wise to wait a few days—until after the First Presidency is formally established—before we have the forensic analysis done?" Both of the others agreed.

When Ririe was alone, he called Bishop Donavan.

"Pat, there's been a new development. That pesky manuscript is now in the possession of the LDS Church. I'll give you the details later. My question now is, do you want to have your experts take another look?"

"If possible, yes, I would like to have another look at the manuscript myself. Could I have it for, say, three days?"

Ririe hesitated for about a second, then responded, "I owe you at least that much, Pat, but can you wait a few days? We'd like to have our expert take one more look. I'll bring it to you personally as soon as I get it back."

"Of course I can wait, Tony."

"I appreciate your friendship and your help. You're a great source of strength to me, Pat, and you're in my prayers every day."

"Tony, I'll be praying for you on your big day Thursday."

Anthony J. Ririe now was not only the de facto President of the Quorum of the Twelve Apostles but also the de facto President of the Church. He asked Hank Cannon to continue as before. And he let Grant Belnap know that he would be the new second counselor.

President Ririe sent word to each of the apostles that the regular meeting of the Twelve would be held on Thursday, July 16, at which time organizing the new First Presidency would be the only matter of business.

Tuesday and Wednesday, July 14 and 15, were a blur of events following the funeral as well as the activities preceding Pioneer Day. Calls, letters, faxes, and other electronic messages had poured in from church and civic leaders all over the world. The President of the United States had called personally, as had many other heads of state. Beverly Moore had a difficult time protecting her boss from visitors, but she had an instinct born of long experience regarding which ones to let through and which to fend off.

On Thursday, July 16, 2020, Anthony J. Ririe was selected by the Twelve to be the next president of the Church. He was ordained a prophet, seer, and revelator and set apart as the President of the Church of Jesus Christ of Latter-day Saints by all of the other Apostles, with Elder Homer Wilcox, the next senior apostle, acting as mouth. The quorum approved Ririe's nominations of Henry Cannon and Grant Belnap as his counselors, and Ririe set them apart. Then the three members of the First Presidency set Elder Homer Wilcox apart as the President of the Quorum of the Twelve.

Before the meeting adjourned, President Ririe reminded the ten remaining members of that august body that there were three vacancies to fill. He asked each of them to provide three nominations no later than Monday morning, July 20th. He also confirmed that there would be another regularly scheduled meeting of the First Presidency and the Quorum of the Twelve on July 30th.

Ririe suggested privately to Belnap that he call Norma and confirm that his new status would not delay their wedding but might call for different honeymoon plans.

That afternoon at a news conference, the new First Presidency was introduced to the world. Local, national, and international television and other newsgathering agencies were represented at that news conference in the Joseph Smith Building, formerly the Hotel Utah.

Rosalie Torres, as head of the church Public Relations Department, introduced Ririe. In turn, Ririe introduced his two counselors, gave a short statement, and opened the news conference to questions.

"What will be your major emphasis?"

"How is the Church doing financially?"

"When will the vacancies in the Quorum of the Twelve be filled?"

"What do you regard as your major challenge?"

Ririe answered each question directly, without evasion, frequently with the insertion of a bit of humor. Then came the last question, which sounded to some of the press like a plant.

"Why do you think the Lord took Elder Edward Hayes when he did, since he would now be the President of the Church had he lived?"

"I can answer that one without any hesitation whatsoever," Ririe responded firmly. "I don't know."

At last the news conference was over. The church principals disappeared through a well-guarded door and made their separate ways to their respective offices. After the usual shots of the reporters on the scene, in which the chief points were repeated, lights, cameras, and recorders were carefully packed away, and old friends in the news business shared their reactions to the news conference.

And the new leaders embarked on their newly defined responsibilities—the most pressing of which was dealing with the manuscript.

"The forensic analysis, Brethren. We used Robert McDonald initially. Is he still the best man for the job?" Ririe ask his counselors.

Both counselors agreed, and McDonald once again was asked to report to President Ririe.

"As I told you when you first asked me to look at it," McDonald repeated, "if this is genuine, Brethren, it'll take me days, maybe weeks to say so. If, on the other hand, it's a fake, I may know much sooner."

"I hope you can finish much of your work in three or four days. I know that's rushing things, but I've promised to let Bishop Donavan have it for a few days when you've had your shot at it. I'll call you as soon as he returns it and you might get more time to examine it. But let me remind you what I declared earlier: it is a fake, Brother McDonald, of that I am certain. Nevertheless, guard it with your life; work on it in total secrecy but with total honesty."

CHAPTER FORTY-FOUR

SETTLING IN

President Ririe moved to James D. Wood's office that hadn't been used for months. Members of the Wood family had already removed his personal mementos. Belnap took Ririe's old office, and Hank Cannon stayed where he had been.

Their secretaries made the move with their bosses, with the exception of Norma Ashcraft, now on paid leave. Her move from a non-dating single woman to the fiancée of a counselor in the First Presidency almost overwhelmed her. After Belnap tried out several temporaries, he chose Sarah Green, who had faithfully served Edward Hayes during his years in the Quorum.

In addition to Beverly Moore, Anthony Ririe retained the male secretary who had served President Wood for the previous ten years. His travels as President of the Church called for a secretary to be nearby at all times, a situation not suitable for a woman.

On July 17th at 8 a.m. and each working day thereafter, Ririe, Cannon, and Belnap met as the First Presidency to handle the myriad details associated with the operation of the very large worldwide and still rapidly growing Church. Always present at those meetings was yet another male secretary, the Secretary to the First Presidency.

The great majority of the details discussed in those meetings, including the highly confidential matters of the financial balance sheet of the Church and cases of Church discipline that reached the highest level on appeal, were never made known outside that room. Exceptions were appointments to and releases from the Quorums of the Seventy, shuffles in assignments of area presidencies and membership of the various committees, as well as calls to new mission presidents.

In many ways, these daily business sessions might have been considered a grind, but to these brethren it was a most sacred trust. It not only gave them personal satisfaction but also brought fulfilling joy.

McDonald returned the manuscript to Ririe as promised and made his report.

"President, two of the three major indicators tell me that the document might well be genuine. The third, provenance, could tip the scales either way. Provenance needs to be examined most carefully but I can't do much from here without knowing more about where the document came from and where it's been for the last two hundred years."

"Thank you, Brother McDonald. Although you say you can't do anything about provenance from here, I'll get the manuscript back to you in three or four days. Then maybe we can dig deeper into this provenance business."

Ririe then called Bishop Donavan and arranged to give him the manuscript that same day. *I wonder what he'll do with it?* Ririe mused.

CHAPTER FORTY-FIVE

AND THEN

The only working days the First Presidency did not meet were when two of them were out of town simultaneously, which happened regularly due to the desire of the top leaders to meet with Church members all over the world. But they were all in town for the next several days because of the impending Belnap/Ashcraft wedding as well as the forthcoming "Days of Forty-Seven" grand parade.

The former took place in the Salt Lake Temple early on the morning of July 23, with President Anthony J. Ririe officiating. A small announcement of the marriage was placed in the local papers from where it was picked up by the news services and made known throughout the world. A modest reception with a very limited guest list was held at the home of the bride's parents. The press of new duties delayed their official honeymoon, but the rest of their life together was one continuous honeymoon. Grant loved her all the more after he got over the shock of belatedly learning his new bride was a stock market whiz.

The big parade on the next day found Anthony Ririe and his wife, Marybeth, riding in the main Church car. Ririe—yielding to pressure from the Twelve and to Marybeth's better judgment—had reluctantly given up the balloon idea. Midway through the parade, Boyd Noorda, Garrick's replacement, answered his cell phone, then handed it to Ririe.

Ross Bingham, the electronics expert, was calling. "In my opinion those tapes had been severely edited."

"What does that mean, Brother Bingham?" President Ririe asked.

"It could easily mean that what appeared to be Elder Hayes's words ordering the theft of the manuscript have been rearranged from their original form to convey the exact reverse—'don't steal the manuscript.'"

"Thank you, Brother Bingham, that is good news. Please arrange to meet with me as soon as your time will permit."

"I'm calling from your outer office with the help of Beverly Moore. I sensed some urgency in this matter, so I flew over this morning."

"Please ask Beverly to get you in as soon as possible."

Ririe returned the phone to Noorda who immediately responded to another call and handed the receiver back to Ririe.

"Sorry to break in on your parade, Tony, but I won't rain on it," Pat Donavan was almost chuckling.

"Sounds curious, Pat. What have you been up to?"

"I got in late last night from a very quick trip to Chicago. Does that city sound familiar to you, Tony? Anyway, I took the manuscript to a former parishioner in the Chicago area, a forensic specialist by the name of Dr. Bernard Horne. Horne immediately recognized the manuscript and quickly told me about having seen the other half and learning from the owner that it was a fake of his own creation. After some discussion, I gave the manuscript to Horne and requested it be returned to the rightful owner. Hope I haven't overstepped my bounds, Tony."

Ririe took a few seconds to think about what he just learned. "Pat, I don't know whether to laugh, to cry, or shout 'Praise the Lord!' No, you didn't overstep your bounds, Pat. I remember you telling me some time ago that you knew a forensic specialist. So the problem is solved and the case is closed. Right?"

"Right."

"Pat, you are the only one in the world who could've done what you just told me. I'll be eternally in your debt. If it wouldn't endanger my eternal salvation, I would say we should get together for a good stiff drink."

"We must get together, Tony, over a steak dinner and try to convert each other," Pat responded.

As Ririe returned the phone to Noorda, he whispered the good news in Marybeth's ear and suggested that she be the one to inform his counselors that "Operation Preemptive Strike" had come to an end.

At about the same time on the 24th, Mitchell Potter and Sherman Drake walked up to the office of Dr. Bernard Horne, the forensic analyst. They debated whether to wait outside for Al Trask, who had notified them that Horne was ready with his report, and had agreed he would meet them there.

When he hadn't arrived fifteen minutes beyond the appointed hour, they entered Horne's office.

"Sit down, gentlemen," Horne ordered briskly. "Mr. Trask won't be joining us this morning, but he asked me to tell you what I've learned. I learned that the document was a forgery within an hour of your leaving this office about two months ago. Mr. Trask informed me of that fact himself when he returned to my office as soon as he was certain you were out of the area. He identified himself as the forger. He told me that he would've told you earlier, but felt that sweating it out for eight weeks was no more than you deserved because of your mishandling of the first part of the document. He asked me to make two requests of you. First, don't try to reach him. Second, should the missing pages be returned to either of you, you are to send them to me, and I'll return them to Mr. Trask. There is no bill because I rendered insignificant services. That's all I have to say, except, good day, gentlemen." Horne chose not to tell them of his visit the previous day from the Catholic Bishop from Salt Lake.

Potter and Drake were too stunned to say anything until they were out the door. It took Drake several days to admit to himself that he had acted hastily and stupidly. *Why did I assume that damn document was genuine? Mitch told me it was, but how did he know?*

Harriet Hudson read of the marriage of Grant Belnap to his secretary, Norma Ashcraft, in the Chicago papers.

"So, he married his secretary. I was his secretary once. Why couldn't I have been the one?"

A few days later her body was discovered by firemen called by neighbors who saw smoke seeping through one of the bedroom windows. Investigators determined the cause of the fire—a smoldering cigarette in the bed. The coroner initially thought she had been overcome by smoke, but he found no evidence of smoke in her lungs other than the accumulated results of years of heavy smoking. He finally reported the cause of death as a mixture of alcohol and barbiturates but was unable to determine if her death was an accident or suicide. Because she had cut off all contact with her living relatives in Salt Lake City years earlier, Drake paid to have her body cremated. The urn containing her ashes rested on a bookshelf in his shared apartment for several months, and then disappeared after a visit from one of his new women.

Robert McDonald met with President Ririe on the afternoon of the parade and started to give Ririe details on what he had told him during the parade, particularly provenance. Ririe cut him off with a broad smile. "Brother McDonald, we've learned through other sources that provenance would take us back only a year or two. Perhaps, after some time has elapsed I will fill you in. For now, all I can do is thank you for your professional efforts."

"President, if I may be so bold, I surely would like to be the one to write up the story when that time comes," McDonald requested

Almost as soon as McDonald left Ririe's office, Ross Bingham came in with a written report that exonerated Ed Hayes and established that someone had tampered with the tapes. The report told of the electronic gaps where words had been omitted.

President Ririe invited Stephanie Hayes to his office where he told her the entire story of her husband's suspected involvement with the manuscript, the confrontation that led to his collapse and death, and the subsequent investigation that cleared him.

Stephanie listened to the whole story, then responded thoughtfully, "That's an absolutely amazing account, President Ririe. I'm glad to have my concerns relieved. Life will go on. The gospel's still true. And I sustain you as a divinely chosen prophet, seer, and revelator with all my heart. May the Lord continue to bless you in your very heavy responsibilities in His kingdom."

Grant and Norma left early in August for a secluded week in Hawaii.

Bishop Patrick J. Donavan continued his faithful service in the Salt Lake Diocese; and Tony and Pat, who loved each other as brothers, continued to meet from time to time and to pray for each other's immortal souls. But they never did get around to having that discussion about their respective views on faith.

Mitch Potter and Sherman Drake remained convinced that somewhere in the world a document existed that would invalidate Joseph Smith's claims regarding the Book of Mormon. That conviction, combined with their hatred of all things connected with the Church of Jesus Christ of Latter-day Saints, became the motivating force that gave them what little meaning there was in their otherwise meaningless existence.

At the October Semi-annual General Conference, Ririe urged the Church membership not only to read but also to study the Book of Mormon. In the moments before he stood to deliver his major address, Tony Ririe thought, *What would I now be saying if that document had been genuine?*

Anthony J. Ririe, Henry Cannon, and Grant Belnap enjoyed a fruitful First Presidency into the second quarter of the twenty-first century. The Church continued to grow in population with the new converts remaining active in greater numbers than ever before. Their presidency also saw more acceptance by other churches.

But they and Marybeth, along with Bishop Donavan and his Book of Mormon-expert priest, carried with them the memories of those three months in the middle of the Year of Our Lord, 2020.

Nothing comparable to that three-month crisis, however, occurred again until the great disaster of 2026. But that is another story.

END NOTES

P. 76. Richard Poll first used the terms Iron-rodders and Liahonas in "What the Church Means to People Like Me," *Dialogue*, 2, no. 4 (Winter 1967): 107-17.

P. 78. Blaise Pascal: *Encyclopedia Britannica* 1993, 25:459.

P. 109. William James, *The Will to Believe* (New York: Longmans, Green and Co., 1898), 29.

P. 111. See Wayne A. Larsen and Alvin C. Rencher, "Who Wrote the Book of Mormon? An Analysis of Wordprints" in *Book of Mormon Authorship: New Light on Ancient Origins*, edited by Noel B. Reynolds (Provo, Utah: Brigham Young University Religious Studies Center, 1982), 157-188.

P. 112. Sterling M. McMurrin, *The Humanist Manifesto and the Future* The Utah Humanist, Vol. 2/No.12, December 1992.

P. 115. Bernice Maher Mooney, *The Story of the Cathedral of the Madeleine* (Salt Lake City: Lithographics, 1981) and her *The Cathedral of the Madeleine* (Salt Lake City: Friends of the Cathedral, 1993).

P. 116. *Catholic Book of Knowledge* (Chicago: Catholic Home Press, 1959) 3:267-71.

P. 148. Ideas related to document authentication were extracted from George J. Throckmorton, "A Forensic Analysis of Twenty-one

Hofmann Documents" in *Salamander* by Linda Sillitoe and Allen Roberts (Salt Lake City: Signature Books, 1988), 533-36.

P. 148. Ideas about the paper gathered from Dard Hunter, *Paper Making: The History and Technique of an Ancient Craft,* 2d ed. (New York, Alfred A. Knopf, 1957).

P. 180. Niccolo Machiavelli, *The Prince,* Great Books of the Western World Series (Chicago: Encyclopedia Britannica,1952) 23:9.

P. 181. "Man proposes, but God disposes," Thomas à Kempis, *Imitation of Christ,* in Bartlett's *Familiar Quotations* 16th ed.. (Boston: Little, Brown and Company):132.

P. 185. Sir Walter Scott, "The Lay of the Last Minstrel," in Bartlett's *Familiar Quotations,* 378.

About the Author

Charles Manley Brown was born in Canada on November 19, 1921, the son of Hugh B. Brown and Zina Young Card Brown. He received his early education in Salt Lake City and secondary education in London, England.

He married Vivienne Grace Bowns in the Salt lake Temple in 1944, and after four years as a co-pilot with American Airlines, earned degrees from Glendale California Community College, the University of Utah, and the University of Southern California, where for thirty years he was a Professor of Education.

Upon his retirement in 1985, he and his wife moved to St. George, Utah, where he has served as Board Member of he Southwest Symphony, President of the Southwest Guild for the Performing Arts, Board Member of the Celebrity Concert Series, Secretary of the Bloomington Hills Home Owners Association, and as a volunteer at Dixie Care and Share. His wife, Grace, a talented organist, accompanist and organizer, has been just as active as Charles in both community and Church.

His Church service has included Member of the Sunday School General Board, Bishop, Counselor in a Stake Presidency, Temple ordinance worker, and Stake Patriarch.

The Browns are the parents of five children with 28 grandchildren and 27 (and counting) great-grandchildren.